"The press doesn't give up easily," Rolf stated. "You wouldn't be a reporter, sneaking around disguised as a secretary, would you?"

Frankie hesitated and then said lightly: "I'm no journalist. I didn't know you suspected me of something."

"You're a woman," Rolf said wryly, "and therefore *always* suspect. . . ."

Romances by
IRIS BROMIGE

ALEX AND THE RAYNHAMS
AN APRIL GIRL
COME LOVE, COME HOPE
THE ENCHANTED GARDEN
THE FAMILY WEB
THE LYDIAN INHERITANCE
THE MASTER OF HERONSBRIDGE
ONLY OUR LOVE
THE TANGLED WOOD
ENCOUNTER AT ALPENROSE
GOLDEN SUMMER
A MAGIC PLACE
APRIL WOOING
A SHELTERING TREE
A HOUSE WITHOUT LOVE

Available in Beagle editions

A MAGIC PLACE

Iris Bromige

BEAGLE BOOKS • NEW YORK

The characters in this book are entirely imaginary
and bear no relation to any living person

Copyright © 1971 by Iris Bromige

All rights reserved

Published by arrangement with Hodder & Stoughton Ltd.

First printing: May 1973

Printed in the United States of America

BEAGLE BOOKS, INC.
201 East 50 Street, New York, NY 10022

CONTENTS

Chapter		page
1	A Change of Direction	1
2	The Falklands	6
3	A Cool Reception	21
4	Cross Threads	28
5	Two Camps	36
6	The Forsaken Garden	46
7	A Truce	57
8	Remembrance of Things Past	62
9	A Party	71
10	A Touch of Glory	78
11	Julie	86
12	Problems	96
13	Crisis	102
14	Comings and Goings	112
15	Postscript	122
16	For the Record	127
17	Mallorca	131
18	The Last Crusade	141

1
A Change of Direction

NICHOLAS BARBURY switched on the windscreen wiper as the rain started again, and decided that motorway driving was the most monotonous way of travelling that he had yet experienced, and that the next time he visited his sister in the Border country he would use the car-carrier train. His companion had been unusually silent or the past half-hour, afflicted probably as he was by the robot-like procession of speeding vehicles whick made one feel somehow de-humanised. But Frankie had seemed a little below par all the weekend.

'Take heart,' he said cheerfully. 'We're not caught up in this to eternity. I've been told of a good hotel for lunch a few miles ahead where we can turn off.'

His sister roused herself.

'Oh, good. Though I seem to have eaten so much solid fare this weekend that a light lunch will be welcome. Those high teas!'

'Need stoking up to cope with the Border climate. Nice old house that, though. I'm glad things have turned out so well for Jenny. She deserved a break. I rather take to Joel.'

'Mmm. And Jenny looked so well and happy. So different from the pale ghost that emerged from that car smash eighteen months ago. I never thought she'd get over the loss of her friends and her career so completely.'

'Must be love,' said Nick with a wry smile.

'Can't help grieving over the waste of her talent, though. She says she'll never be able to play the piano again. Her hand's recovered hardly any of its flexibility.'

'Well, she seems as happy as a lark at burying herself in domesticity, so why should we worry? Anyway, good pianists aren't exactly thin on the ground, and it's a tough life. Must say I found the weekend reassuring.'

'Me, too. A house-warming party that warmed all of us. They were both so happy and confident that it spilt over on everybody else, too. That house seemed a citadel. I really felt quite reluctant to leave it and face London again.'

'Prospects dim?'

'Extremely.'

'I thought you seemed a bit subdued. Here's our escape route. Let's see what a bottle of wine with our lunch will do for morale.'

He turned off the motorway into a lane which wound along for about a mile to a village, on the fringe of which was a white country-house hotel. A blazing fire welcomed them in the hall. They had two sherries while they toasted their toes and studied the menu which the waiter brought them. That done, and lunch ordered, Nick leaned back in his armchair and surveyed his younger sister with thoughtful eyes. In a family more remarkable for their detachmnt from each other than any close emotional ties, there had always been a special bond of sympathy between Nicholas, the eldest child, and Frances, the youngest of the three. He had never seen her lively spirit so quenched before. She was too thin, and the heart-shaped face showed hollows under the high cheekbones which he had never noticed before. The long record of failure was leaving its mark. As though sensing his train of thought, she said abruptly, 'I think I'm going to throw it up, Nick.'

'Your career, you mean?'

'Career? Two microscopic parts in the three years since I left the Academy. Acting's an overcrowded profession now, and I suppose I simply haven't enough talent.'

'You need a good deal of luck, too. And the right contacts.'

'Perhaps. Anyway, I'm tired of living from hand to mouth, taking all sorts of odd jobs to keep going, and pestering the agents. I think I ought to cut my losses and tackle something else if I'm not to feel a permanent failure.'

'A pity to waste your training.'

'I know. But I have to face the facts. During the past three years, I've spent eight weeks doing the job I was trained for and the rest being a shop assistant, a temporary clerk, an art gallery attendant and a stable girl. Oh, and a post office sorter at Christmas.'

'A wide experience,' observed Nick, grinning.

'Not very satisfying, though.'

'You're only just twenty-one. Not many people make the grade in acting as young as that.'

'But there are so many out of work. I see them at the agents and talk to them. I know that the chance of my getting anywhere is about one in fifty. I'm not prepared to waste my life just hoping, with the odds so much against me. I'm not outstanding. And this way of life is getting me down.'

Nick was silent for a few minutes while he digested this. She had certain assets for the career she had chosen: an attractive, slightly husky voice, a petite but beautifully balanced figure, a lively, expressive face. Not pretty, or goodlooking in the classical sense, but striking colouring with that creamy skin, short black hair and large greeny-blue eyes, and a suggestion of the gamin about her which was appealing. He rather suspected that she was not tough enough for such a highly competitive profession, though. Or patient enough.

'Any other ideas about what you might like to do, then?' he said at last.

'Not really. Except that I'd like to get right away from London for a bit. Seeing Jenny's house this weekend has given me a yen for the simple life, too. London isn't the glamorous place I once thought it.'

'How would you like the Welsh mountains? They're remote enough, and Wales can boast country every bit as lovely as the Scottish border in my opinion. I know of a job going in central Wales. Might do for a stop-gap while you sort yourself out.'

'Tell me more.'

'I was down there the week before last, trying to get an interview with a man called Trevor Falkland. He was a well-known man of letters in the thirties and forties. Better known in America than here. Then he suddenly stopped writing and vanished from the literary scene. No need to bore you with details, but I found out that he was living in Wales, and I thought he was just the person to interview for our "Forgotten Authors" series. I came across a book of his a few years ago and liked it so much that I tracked down two more. Haunting, sensitive novels, with an idyllic flavour. And it intrigued me that he'd stopped writing at his peak, when he was still quite young. I sent Lennox for the interview, but he got nowhere. So I went down myself, thinking that my superior charm might succeed where he'd failed.'

'And did it?'

'Only with Mrs. Falkland. Of the once famous author himself, I got not a glimpse. He refuses to see any journalists. He had a stroke five years ago which left him crippled. That's all I was able to glean from the charming and sympathetic Mrs. Falkland, who didn't seem to realise that her husband had ever been an established writer. She's his second wife and a good deal younger than he is. He never talks about the years before he met her, and hasn't written a word for publication in the eighteen years of their marriage. That seems to me incredible. Writing' in your blood or it isn't. And it was certainly in Trevor Falksland's all those years ago.'

'And so,' prompted Frankie as Nick paused reflectively.

'Before I left, Mrs. Falkland said that her health not being exactly robust, she would like to find a young woman able to act as a kind of secretary for her husband and companion for her seventeen-year-old daughter, and if I knew of anybody who might like a comfortable home in the country and few duties except just to be around, perhaps I'd let her know. Somebody capable, but young. She doesn't like old people around her, and she thinks her husband would benefit from having a young person around too. I didn't give it another thought until now, being a bit cheesed off at failing to get the interview. But it's a fine old house in glorious country, and you might like to think about it. When you're at a turning-point, it can help to get right away to a different environment for a bit. You can view things with more detachment. See them in a clearer light.'

'Well, I've nothing to lose, and the beginning of a new year is the right time to make a change. I feel that if I go on any longer hanging about the agents with my begging bowl, I'll lose the last shreds of what little self-respect and confidence remain. I hate to be beaten, though,' she concluded, sighing.

'You're not admitting defeat by taking a breather. Just giving yourself a chance to draw up the balance sheet.'

'A kind heart beats under that blasé exterior of yours, brother,' said Frankie, smiling.

'I have my softer moments. Anyway, this may turn out to be a flop. I know nothing more about it than I've told you. If I were you, I'd go down and stay at a hotel there for a few days and spy out the land. If the place appeals, you can present yourself at Riverdale, that's the name of the Falkland home, with a letter of introduction from yours truly. The hotel I stayed at was quite comfortable.'

'Thanks. I'll do that. And that's enough about my troubles. How's the magazine going?'

'As well as any magazine devoted to the arts can be expected to do. We keep our heads above water. I'm doing book reviews for a daily now, too, which helps.'

'It's funny, you know, how we three, Jenny, you and I, all plunged into artistic careers with high hopes and great zeal, and have all been frustrated. Jenny because of her accident, me because I suppose I'm just not good enough for the stiff competition, and you having to turn journalist because you can't get a book published.'

'And the name of Barbury is destined to be unknown in the worlds of music, drama and letters. We'd make good subjects for a Chekov play. But comfort yourself with the example of Jenny. There are other fields to conquer,' said Nick with gentle mockery.

'You, at least, are nearer your target than any of us, using the tools of your choice, words.'

'To misquote G.B.S., those who can, write; those who can't, criticise. The waiter's signalling that lunch is ready. Let's fortify our souls with some food. The combination of motorway driving in heavy traffic on a wet day in January and the realisation of failed ambitions calls for the best available burgundy to sustain us. And no pecking at your food. If I stand a girl lunch, I expect her to eat it with hearty enjoyment.'

They were both in good spirits again by the time they had reached their coffee.

'That was a splendid meal, Nick. Bless you. I feel a new woman. Haven't eaten such a good curry since I was last at Grandma's. It's put me in a confident mood. I shall go to Wales to seek a change of fortune.'

'All on a couple of glasses of burgundy and curried chicken. Remind me to lend you my copy of George Borrow's *Wild Wales*. He writes beautifully of that part of the country. Give you some idea of what you're going to.'

'I'm much obliged, Nick. For everything.'

'Don't thank me. May be a wild goose chase I'm sending you on. But if you do want the job and get it, you might be able to find out more about Trevor Falkland for me. I'm intrigued by the man.'

'You wouldn't be planting me as a spy?'

'Nothing further from my mind. But if you could use your influence to get me an interview, or find out anything that would help to satisfy my curiosity, I'd welcome it, of course.'

'Of course,' said Frankie sweetly, her head on one side and her eyes teasing him.

Nick grinned, and until the motorway claimed them again, talked about George Borrow's travels.

2
The Falklands

THE hotel which her brother had recommended was of a grander variety than Frankie had anticipated, and although she was delighted with its peaceful position and its comfort, she could not afford to stay there for more than a few days. Enjoying an excellent dinner on her first night, she decided to have a look round the country the next day, find the Falkland home and, if it appealed to her, telephone for an appointment as soon as possible.

The large dining-room was fairly full on that Saturday night, which surprised her at that time of the year until she realised that many of the diners were not hotel residents but had merely come in for dinner. There were two parties, one all-male, obviously a club of some sort, on the far side of the room, and one smaller family party seated at a table just in front of her. For lack of anything better to do between the courses, she found herself studying this party with some interest, and since the table was quite close and the diners in an uninhibited mood, she could hear enough of their conversation to glean a few facts.

The party numbered nine in all and was celebrating the sixtieth birthday of the man in a wheel-chair at the head of the table. He was a heavily built man with a square, rugged face and thick white hair. His skin was the colour of old parchment and his face deeply lined. One side of his mouth was pulled down a little, and he looked years older than sixty. He seemed to be taking little part in the conversation, listening with an air of faint amusement but giving the impression of being a spectator rather than the object of the celebration. There were two other men of his own generation, one round and jolly, who sat with his back to her so that she could only see his bald pate, and the other opposite him who was shorter and firmer of build and who surveyed his food with deep suspicion and a pugnacious expression. Also with their backs to her were a sandy-haired young man called Barry, with a lively tongue and an infectious laugh, a girl in a red dress with beautiful ash-blonde hair which shone like silk, and a middle-aged woman with dark hair streaked with grey who wore a blue silk dress and who looked after the crippled man on her right with quiet solicitude.

On the other side of the table and facing Frankie was the tall dark man of about thirty who had proposed the toast to the old man at the beginning of the proceedings, and who was now talking to the girl beside him. When he had first stood up, glass in hand, perfectly at ease, to convey their best wishes to his father on the attainment of his sixtieth birthday, Frankie's reactions had been mixed. She approved of his deep voice which would have been a boon to an actor, and recognised a powerful personality. But there was something cold and ruthless, even a suggestion of cruelty, in that brown-skinned face with the long straight nose, dark eyes and dense black hair. A curiously shuttered face, giving away nothing but a latent strength, as though he watched the world with wary, assessing eyes, expecting it to be rough, and ready to deal with it. A little smile in response to something his companion said softened his expression slightly but he reminded her too much of that brutal producer of the last play she had appeared in who had torn her to shreds for her performance, small as it had been, and had finally wrecked all her self-confidence as an actress. He had been tall and very dark, too, but with coarser features than this man, and a cruel, mocking tongue. But common to both was the cold, assessing eye. With a shiver, Frankie turned her attention to his companion, a brown-haired girl in her teens with a smile which redeemed her unpretentious looks. The ninth member of the party presided at the other end of the table, and Frankie found her appearance altogether captivating. She supposed her to be in her thirties; a fragile-looking woman with fair hair and an apple-blossom complexion who was listening to the young man called Barry with her head on one side, an affectionate smile on her lips. She was wearing a grey silk suit and reminded Frankie of a piece of Dresden china.

Her survey was interrupted by the arrival of her waiter with a *charlotte russe* and while she gave her attention to this, she ruminated on the relationship of the members of the party. There seemed no marked family likeness to help her. The dark-haired woman in the blue silk dress was probably the crippled man's wife. The other two elderly men perhaps his brothers, but she was unable to sort out the young people, and the Dresden-china lady seemed in a class of her own. Surely not the son's wife. He was now lifting his glass to the sandy-haired young man.

'Congratulations on passing your finals, Barry,' he said. 'Another qualified surveyor in the business is more than welcome.'

'Thanks, Rolf,' said Barry cheerfully. 'I shall expect a handsome salary now, of course.'

'When I was first qualified,' began the pugnacious looking man, but his voice was drowned in the laughter of the younger members of the party and it was obvious that Barry had been trailing his coat for this reaction.

It was soon after that when Frankie, shifting her attention from the Dresden-china lady to the other end of the table, found the dark eyes of Rolf studying her calmly. As her eyes met his, she could guess their message. After a moment, she lowered her eyes to the last morsel of her *charlotte russe,* feeling uncomfortable. She supposed her interest had seemed a bit blatant, but when dining on your own, who could resist eavesdropping? When she glanced up again, he was still surveying her through narrowed eyes as though daring her to continue her role of inquisitive spectator. She flushed, stooped to collect her handbag and walked out of the dining-room to a far corner of the adjoining lounge, where the waiter brought her coffee.

When the party came into the lounge a little later, the round, jolly man was leading them towards her end of the room until Rolf, wheeling the invalid chair, diverted them to the far corner from her. Away from prying eyes and ears, she thought, fixing her attention on a magazine she had picked up. There was a good deal of laughter and chatter from them. The men's club had gone into a far room where some sort of a lecture seemed to be taking place. A few middle-aged couples were scattered about the large lounge. Frankie felt a little lonely and wished Nick were there to keep her company. Rolf passed her once on his way to the cocktail bar, and returned a few minutes later with a tray of drinks. She kept her eyes riveted on her magazine when he passed, only looking up when his back was to her. He moved well and obviously went to a good tailor. They had needed a man with a presence like that for Iago instead of that weedy little man who, with all his acting ability, had seemed to diminish the character and turn that large-scale villain into a petty spiv. This man had just the right suggestion of mocking cruelty behind the smooth mask. But thinking of that only reminded her of their producer again and she could still wince at the recollection of his opinion of her Bianca. A tongue like a flail on her naked flesh.

Driven by this painful recollection to seek distraction in the television lounge, she found the newsreel depressing and the play that followed squalid and pointless. When she passed through the main lounge again on her way to bed, the party had gone.

She felt in better spirits the next morning when the grey drizzle of the previous day had been succeeded by crisp bright weather, and she took a packed lunch and set off to explore the country nearby. She started off along a path beside a mountain torrent in full spate after the winter rains. The path climbed up through woods which sloped down to the stream. On her left and below her, the swirling, foaming water thundered along over boulders on its serpentine course between the wooded banks, while on her right tall trunks of oak and beech reared high above her, and a pleasing pattern of sunshine and shadow played over them and enriched the carpet of last autumn's leaves on the ground below.

It was nearly midday when the path brought her to a narrow rustic bridge and a fine waterfall of about eighty feet split into two halves by a rocky ledge across it. With a wooden seat conveniently placed to view the waterfall, she decided to eat her lunch there. It was some little time before she could bring herself to the mundane task of investigating the greaseproof-wrapped packages, for there was a magical quality about the waterfall that was almost hypnotic. The highest stretch of the fall had a glassy smoothness until it hit the ledge with cascades of white spray gleaming in the sun before it tumbled down over rocky bulges to the river below. The steep rocky sides of the ravine were covered with moss, ferns and grass, and overhung by oak trees. Some ivy, swarming up the trunk of one of these, glittered with drops like diamonds where the sun caught the leaves wet with spray. Far below, at the foot of the ravine, wild rhododendrons grew thickly.

Sitting on the seat, the thunderous music of the waterfall in her ears, it was as though she had the world to herself, and a grand mood of exaltation came over her. Nick had been right, she thought. This was what she needed. A complete change of scene, an interval away from it all so that she could see the past in perspective and make up her mind whether her decision to give up all hopes of an acting career was final, and if so, to decide on a new path. Just now, her old life seemed a world away and no finger beckoned her back.

It was too cold to sit there for long, beautiful as it was, and after she had eaten ham sandwiches, an apple and a banana, she pushed on up the path, now on the other side of the river. After about an hour's uphill walking, she emerged from the wood on to the lower slopes of the mountain with an unpronounceable name, the upper stony reaches of which would demand climbing boots and stern effort. After surveying its majestic contours for a few minutes, she decided that it was time to turn back. Trying to find a different way back, she lost herself, and it was nearly dark when she scrambled wearily down a stony track to the village and trudged the last mile back to the hotel, so that any idea of seeing the home of the Falklands that day was given up.

Before going into breakfast the next morning, she asked the porter if he knew where Riverdale was.

'About a mile or more up the river valley, miss. Best take the bus from the village post office and get off at Ash Corner. You'll see the entrance a few yards on. The bus leaves on the hour.'

She thanked him and caught the ten o'clock bus. It was a bright, cold morning again, and her mood of optimism prevailed as the bus trundled along the narrow twisting lane, picking up a few passengers, all of whom were known by name to the cheerful driver who also collected the fares. Her plan of a preliminary survey of the Falkland home was complicated by the fact that it was totally obscured from the lane. The wide entrance gates merely revealed a long curving drive between tall trees and overgrown shrubs. She hesitated, then opened the gate and walked up the drive. She could probably get a view of the house from the curve. But that curve led only to another, and it took her several minutes before she emerged from the belt of woodland to see the house, a large, square, grey stone building fronted by a wide terrace and behind it neglected lawns sloping down to a river which wound through a thin scattering of trees.

The sound of car wheels on the drive sent her back hastily into the shelter of a clump of laurels, for she felt a trespasser. As the car swung round the house, she pushed back into the woods and, hampered by ivy and brambles and brushwood, made her way back to the gates with ruined stockings and a scratched leg. She had seen enough, however, to make her telephone Mrs. Falkland as soon as she arrived back at the hotel, and an appointment was fixed for that afternoon.

She supposed that the woman who let her in was the housekeeper, a dour, grey-haired woman wearing a nylon housecoat. About as welcoming as a slab of granite, thought Frankie, as she was conducted through the large oak-panelled hall to the sitting-room.

'Miss Barbury, Mrs. Falkland,' said the woman abruptly, and left them.

And Frankie found herself facing the Dresden-china lady of the hotel party, and being greeted with a heart-warming smile.

'Let me take your coat, and sit down by the fire. It's really cold today, isn't it?' she said in a light, pretty voice.

Frankie gave her Nick's note of introduction and watched her while she read it. She was a little older than Frankie had guessed when she had seen her at the party, but surely not old enough to be the wife of the crippled man and mother of a seventeen-year-old daughter. Slender, petite, with fair skin and regular features, wearing a beautifully cut pale blue jersey dress, she was altogether delightful to look at.

'How kind of your brother to respond to my S.O.S. so promptly! Such a handsome young man, with the most charming manners. Not my idea of a journalist at all. I found him a most agreeable companion, and was sorry I couldn't help him. Now he rewards my inability to help him with this introduction. I call that generous.'

'Well, it was just chance that I'd come to a sort of crossroads. A complete change of work seemed indicated. Of course, I may not be suitable for the sort of job you have in mind for me. I've had no secretarial experience.'

'Tell me about yourself,' said Mrs. Falkland, settling into her armchair and studying Frankie with a sympathetic expression which invited confidence.

'Not much to tell. I was trained at R.A.D.A. for a stage career, and only succeeded in getting two small parts in three years. I made out by taking odd jobs. But I've got to face the fact that acting's an overcrowded profession, I'm not specially talented, and I'm not prepared to go grubbing along like this any longer. When I told Nick that I'd decided to cut my losses and start something new, he suggested that I might like to come and see you.'

'Well, that puts a special bond of sympathy between us, my dear, because I was an actress, too, before I married. Oh, not exactly famous. Minor parts in musicals. I might have got somewhere if I'd gone on, but I married when I was twenty-six, my daughter arrived within a year, and I felt I was of more value at home. And I may add that I've no regrets, only a few little hankerings now and again for London and the stage. What parts did you play?'

'Bianca in *Othello* in London and Rosalie in *Lady Windermere's Fan* in a provincial tour.'

'The classics. You might have done better in lighter-weight works.'

'I'd have tried anything after the first year, although I always wanted most to play in Shakespeare, but there was simply too much competition.'

'And you're not a thruster, I can see. I wasn't, either. But I had good friends. However, your bad luck may be my good fortune now. Are you sure you want to bury yourself in this quiet country, though?'

'It will be a complete change. But what would be wanted of me?'

'Your brother will have told you about my poor husband. A stroke five years ago left him partially paralysed. I've tried to act as secretary and companion to him as far as possible, but I owe it to my daughter not to neglect her, and I have to keep an eye on my mother who lives in London. I'm not as strong as I'd like to be, so it would be an enormous help to me to have a young assistant to stand in for me. If you could type or write my husband's letters for him, read to him sometimes, and wheel him out in the garden when the weather's inviting, it would free me to go to London more often to see my mother, whose health is failing. As it is, I worry about leaving my husband and Julie here with Mrs. Filey their only companion. A young person like you would be such an asset to them both; cheer them up. And cheer me up, too,' she concluded with a smile.

'Well, it doesn't seem a difficult job. I ought to be able to cope with those duties.'

'But you'll want to know what we can offer you besides duties. A good deal of free time, but not, alas, much entertainment for young people. Plenty of good riding and walking, of course. And Marlbury is only fifteen miles away, with a reasonable bus service from the village. It's a pleasant town with some good shops and a concert hall and theatre. Do you drive?'

'No. I've never earned enough money to buy a car, and as

I've lived away from home ever since I left school, there's been no opportunity to use the family car.'

'We'll get a bicycle for you, then, if you accept the post. We sold our car after my husband's stroke, and I make use of the services of a very nice little car-hire man in the village. He's not expensive, and most obliging. For all that, you may find it a dull life after London.'

'I don't think so. My parents live in a rural part of Surrey and I've always liked the country. London hasn't seemed exactly glamorous these past years, and it can be a lonely place.'

'You may miss it more than you expect if you come here. But why should I discourage you?' added Mrs. Falkland gaily. 'And it's time I discussed salary, and holidays. And showed you the house and what would be your room if you decide to come. I'm afraid I'm not at all business-like. First, though, I'll ask Mrs. Filey to bring us some tea.'

Over tea, Mrs. Falkland offered what seemed to Frankie a reasonable salary, and filled in more of the family picture.

'Julie's at school. We're great friends, but she's just at the difficult age now. Neither child nor woman. I'm sure she'd welcome a companion like you. This old house is a little gloomy for the girl, I feel. Her father's health can't but put a damper on things. We don't entertain much, and then only the Falkland relations, whom Julie finds a dull lot, I'm afraid.'

Frankie had not mentioned her view of the family party at the hotel as Mrs. Falkland had given no evidence of having seen her before, but it had not struck her as a dull family.

'Do they live near?' she asked.

'Yes. At Mynelly, a mile or two down the valley. The Falklands are builders. Own a big business with offices in Marlbury and works just outside. Been the family business for several generations. My husband plays no part in it now, of course. It's managed by his two brothers and his son by his first marriage.'

That would be Iago, thought Frankie, and he seemed to be the only snag she had come across, but with her next words Mrs. Falkland reduced the snag considerably.

'Rolf, my husband's son, comes here quite often, but lives in a cottage a few miles away which he inherited from old Mr. Falkland. I thought he would come back here after his father had the stroke. But it was not to be. Quite understandable. He has his own life to live and has always been very independent. He worked in London for a few years, then when his father had the stroke, he returned to Wales and joined the firm, but chose to live in a flat in Marlbury until he inherited the cottage. But he's fond of his father and keeps an eye on his business affairs for him. Now, is there anything else you would like to know? You will be living here, after all, and mustn't accept the job unless you feel you would be happy here.'

'I think I should, but perhaps Mr. Falkland ought to see me. I might not suit him.'

'I've little fear of that, and I know he'll accept my judgment when I tell him I've found the perfect answer to my problem.'

'Perfect?' said Frankie, smiling. 'Isn't that putting it a bit high?'

'Not a bit of it,' said Mrs. Falkland. 'This is my lucky day, and I bless fate for bringing that handsome brother of yours to our house that day. Now come along and I'll show you round. Then we can look in on my husband for a few minutes, but we won't stay longer as he's very tired today. We had a family party to celebrate his sixtieth birthday on Saturday, and he hasn't really recovered from it yet. There's just one thing. My husband has a great dislike of publicity and the press in any shape or form. I think it would be as well not to say anything about your brother. He won't connect your name, because the young man who first came was a Mr. Lennox, and I didn't mention your brother's visit to him because I knew it would only upset him, and nothing would make him give an interview. So I think, dear, we'll just forget your connection with that magazine, and never mention it to anybody. I'll say you saw the advertisement I put in *The Times*. Which brought absolutely no applicants, I may add. A little white lie, but harmless, and justified by the need not to disturb Trevor's peace of mind. He has so much to endure, poor darling. You agree?'

'Of course.'

'Now let me take you on a little tour of the house. I've made it as bright and cosy as I can, but these large old country houses are far from ideal to live in.'

To Frankie, however, after the poky little bed-sitting room which had been her home for the past year, the large lofty rooms, wide staircase, and windows with fine views, stood for a more spacious life where one could breathe, expand, know privacy and feel the call of wide horizons. The room suggested for her use was at least four times the size of her London bed-sitter, and its circular bay window occupied the whole of one side and looked across the garden and the river valley to a range of mountains, the higher peaks of which were snow-covered. It was attractively furnished with dark oak furniture, flowered chintz curtains and a pale green carpet with a pattern of gold roses on it. Frankie found it charming, and said so.

'A little old-fashioned, but then this is an old-fashioned house, and I've given up attempts to modernise it,' said Mrs. Falkland.

Her husband's study was on the ground floor at the back of the house, and Frankie went in with some trepidation, for Mrs. Falkland had made her husband sound a little formidable, and her own recollection of him tallied with this. He was sitting in his wheel-chair at a desk in the window, papers in front of him, a tray of tea on a low table beside him.

'Darling, I've brought Miss Barbury to see you. I hope it isn't inconvenient. I think I've nearly persuaded her to come to our aid.'

'I've always admired your powers of persuasion, my dear Caroline. She could charm the bark off a tree, Miss Barbury, so be on your guard,' said Trevor Falkland as he took Frankie's outstretched hand and gave her a searching look from under his shaggy eyebrows.

Frankie smiled and took the chair he indicated. He had a fine head, but the big frame looked wasted and his dark suit hung loosely on him. The pallor of his face, the deep lines scored on it and the distortion of his mouth gave an even more forbidding effect than had been apparent under the soft lights of the hotel dining-room. It was a ravaged face, acquainted with pain, which in some vague way shocked her. She watched him while Mrs. Falkland was telling him about her, and found it hard to believe that this grim old man was the husband of her Dresden-china lady who seemed little older than Frankie herself and as out of place in this whole setting as a lily on the bare slopes of a Welsh mountain.

'So you see, darling, what an asset Miss Barbury would be here, for all of us,' concluded Caroline Falkland, putting a hand on her husband's shoulder and smiling down at him.

'Quite. But you're young to bury yourself in this quiet spot,' he said, keeping his eyes on Frankie. 'This rebound from urban life may be too drastic. You see it as an escape?'

'Not exactly. I've failed in one sphere. I need to find another.'

'I doubt whether this job would satisfy any ambitions.'

'I'm not ambitious. Perhaps that was the trouble,' said Frankie lightly.

'Hmm. Maybe. As well as talent, you need a certain ruthless egoism to succeed in a competitive sphere. You've given up early, though. How old are you?'

'Just twenty-one. And three years of failure is enough, if it's not to get permanently ingrained.'

'Well, you seem a sensible girl. And Caroline has set her heart on you, I can see. I suggest you come for a three months' trial. If you can put up with us for that length of time, I shall conclude that acting is a more disagreeable profession than I thought,' he added with a dry little smile.

'Now I'm not going to let you paint such a pessimistic picture of us,' said Caroline gaily. 'We're a very happy little family, and you're not the ogre you like to suggest. But you're tired. We'll leave you in peace. Shall I ask Mrs. Filey to bring your dinner in here tonight? When you're tired, I know Julie's prattle gets on your nerves, and there are some pop records on the radio tonight which she wants to listen to, and which I know will not be to your taste.'

'As you wish, my dear. *Au revoir,* Miss Barbury. I shall be pleased if you come here, but think it over carefully.'

He nodded, dismissing her, and she left with Mrs. Falkland, feeling a little disconcerted.

'Ah, that sounds like Julie. I was hoping she'd come while you were here. Julie darling, don't disappear into your room,' called Mrs. Falkland as a girl's back was about to vanish up the stairs. 'I've someone I want you to meet. Come into the sitting-room.'

'Can't I change first?'

'No, darling. Miss Barbury will be leaving soon.'

'O.K. Be down in a sec.'

'Julie can never wait to get out of her school uniform,' explained her mother as they returned to the fire. 'I don't blame her. It's very unbecoming.'

When Julie came in, Frankie recognised the ash-blonde hair which had gone with the red dress in the hotel. Then she had worn it loose, but now it was tied back with a flat bow, and in her green skirt and white blouse with a green and white tie she looked years younger than the girl in the hotel. She had her mother's fair complexion and grey-blue eyes, but lacked the classic features which made Caroline Falkland so outstandingly pretty. Julie's features were a little sharp, and her mouth too small, but she was tall and slender and quite without the gaucherie of adolescence. She greeted Frankie with a smile and seemed pleased at the idea of her coming to live with them.

'There now, you see. We all want you,' said Mrs. Falkland. 'You will give us a trial, won't you?'

She was very appealing just then, with her head on one side, one arm linked in her daughter's.

'Yes, I'd like to.'

'Splendid! Now how soon can you come?'

'In two weeks' time. I have to give a week's notice to my landlady, and I'd like to spend a week with my parents before I come.'

'That's settled, then. We're all going to be the best of friends. I feel it in my bones. My intuition never fails me. And no more Mrs. Falkland. I'm Caroline. Caro to Julie. There's no formality here, and I like to be included in the young generation. That means no Miss Barbury, either. What is your Christian name, dear?'

'Frances. But I'm always called Frankie.'

'Frankie it is, then.'

'Look out. Here comes Frigid Filey,' whispered Julie as footsteps could be heard.

'Naughty,' said her mother, shaking her head but smiling as the housekeeper came into the room and asked if they had finished with the tea-trolley.

'Yes, thank you, Mrs. Filey. Julie will come and fetch what she wants if you'll make another pot of tea for her. And Mr. Falkland will have his dinner in his room tonight.'

'Very well.'

When the housekeeper had closed the door behind her, Julie pulled a face, saying, 'If Mrs. Filey ever smiled, the roof would fall in.'

'We must make allowances, dear,' said her mother. 'She's very conscientious and hard-working, and devoted to your father. Mrs. Filey's been in the service of the Falkland family all her life,' she explained to Frankie. 'She came to us after old Mr. Falkland died and has been a great help to me. You mustn't take any notice of her flinty manner. She's a sterling character underneath.'

'Oh Caro, you know she's a miserable old puritan,' said Julie.

'More tolerance, Julie,' said her mother lightly.

Julie gave her mother an odd little smile and then left them, saying that she couldn't stand her school uniform another minute. Caroline saw Frankie off, and her obvious delight at her acceptance of the post was so reassuring that Frankie walked down the drive happy and confident about this new life in front of her. Caroline Falkland was a delightful person. It would be a pleasure to help her in any way.

Half-way at the gate, a grey car passed her and she thought she recognised Rolf Falkland, but it was growing dark and she could not be sure. The air was bitingly cold as she waited at the bus stop. A bus was due in five minutes, and she turned up her coat collar and stamped her feet to keep warm. She had waited nearly fifteen minutes when she saw the grey car turn out of the drive of Riverdale. It drew up at the bus stop and the driver leaned across and wound down the window. When she heard the voice, she knew it was Rolf Falkland.

'Can I give you a lift to the village?'

'That's very kind of you, but the bus is due.'

'Afraid not. It went about twenty minutes ago and there won't be another for a long time.'

'Are you sure? I looked up the time-table today and it said five-thirty.'

'That's right. It's now five-fifty.'

'My watch must have been slow. Thank you, then. I'd be glad of a lift.'

He had opened the door, and this brought the interior lights on so that she saw him clearly, and he saw her, for his eyebrows went up as he said, 'So you're Miss Barbury, are you?'

As she closed the door, the lights went out leaving only the dim dashboard light, for which she was relieved. She hadn't much liked his searching look, and gave him a brief affirmative to his question.

'Well, I don't have to introduce myself, since I'm sure you got us all lined up quite accurately at the Woolpack Hotel last Saturday night,' he went on drily and she was glad he could not see her flush.

'I had no idea that you were the family offering the post I was interested in until I saw Mrs. Falkland today.'

'Just a coincidence, then?'

'Yes.'

'You're staying at the hotel?'

'Yes. I leave tomorrow morning.'

'Right. I'll drop you off there, then. It's a steep pull up from the village.'

'Thank you.'

He let in the clutch and they moved off.

'My father tells me that you come from London and that this is quite a new sort of job for you,' he said calmly.

'Yes.'

'Did you just see the advertisement or did you hear of it through Mrs. Falkland's London grapevine?'

'London grapevine?' she asked, stalling for time.

'My stepmother has a good many friends in London, including one who runs an employment agency.'

'Didn't Mrs. Falkland tell you that I'd come in answer to the advertisement?' said Frankie, unwilling to lie to him but remembering her promise to say nothing about Nick.

'I only saw her for a few moments just now. Were you the person lurking in the drive this morning?'

'You're beginning to make me feel like a criminal, Mr. Falkland. Yes, I was in the drive. I wanted to have a look at the house before I committed myself to an interview. After all, if it was to be my home, it was no use applying for the job if I didn't like the idea of living there.'

'Very prudent of you. I always like to get the lie of the land myself.'

For all his calm tone, suspicion and hostility lay between them like a sword. Puzzled and riled by his attitude, she remained silent as he drove through the village and turned off up the steep hill to the hotel, battling with her natural inclination always to have things out, for Rolf Falkland was a formidable opponent and her own lively temper had landed her in trouble before. She thanked him with excessively formal politeness when he drew up outside the hotel.

'Not at all, Miss Barbury. I'm glad to have been of service,' he said, with the note of irony robbing his words of any kindness. He had switched on the interior lights and was regarding her with an intentness which she did not like.

'You don't think I'm the right candidate for this job, do you?' she said abruptly, unable to resist the challenge of that look.

'Certain aspects of it puzzle me, I must confess.'

'Such as?'

'Why a young actress from London should want a job of this kind. Why she should show such interest in the family before, as she claims, she knew their identity. Why, if she professes to be an out of work actress in need of a job, she is staying at the most expensive hotel for miles. Why she should spy out the land before applying. There are quite rational explanations for all these points, I'm sure. But together, they remain a little puzzling.'

'With such a suspicious nature, life must seem full of traps, Mr. Falkland. Happily, Mrs. Falkland was more than satisfied with my credentials, and as it is she who is employing me, that's all that matters.'

'As you say,' he replied with a silky note in his voice. 'I shall be interested to see how you make out.'

'Goodnight,' said Frankie angrily, and slid out of the car and ran up the steps of the hotel without a backward glance.

3
A Cool Reception

FRANKIE, recounting her impressions to Nick over a cup of coffee in a café a few evenings later, said, 'The only snag is Rolf Falkland, but he doesn't live there and I hope we shan't see much of him. I had a feeling that Mrs. Falkland found him a difficult character, but she's too sweet-natured to run anybody down. I simply can't see why he should be so suspicious of me, though.'

'No,' said Nick thoughtfully. 'Are you sure you really want this job, Frankie? You'll be on your own, miles from any of us.'

'Don't you think I can look after myself?' she said, smiling and a little surprised at Nick's observation. 'I've been doing it for some years, after all, and the acting profession isn't exactly a nursery school, I can tell you.'

'Well, you have your own sort of armour, perhaps. And you don't have to stay if you don't like it. But there seems a faint suggestion of something fishy about that household, from what you say. I'd hate to be the one who let you in for more trouble.'

'Not to worry. I'm looking forward to it. A challenge. And I think Caroline needs some support, with a stepson like that as well as a stricken and very grim husband to contend with. It's like Beauty and the Beast. I admire her for her gaiety and courage. She's not very strong, you know. *And* she has an ogress of a housekeeper, who's been with the family for years, and probably resents the second young wife.'

'She might be the one who knows what happened to Trevor Falkland to make him go into obscurity. I'm really curious about that. Think you can gain her confidence?'

'As well tap a piece of granite.'

'Well, the old man himself may throw some light on it if you're going to work for him. A nice sympathetic young girl like you may tempt him to unburden himself.'

'I can't pry into what isn't my business, Nick.'

'Of course not. But if anything comes your way that throws light on old Falkland's past, I'd be very interested. And if there's any way of getting him to relent about giving me an interview, I'd be delighted. He intrigues me.'

'I can't do that, Nick. Officially, you and I are not connected,' said Frankie, and told him about Caroline Falkland's wishes in that connection.

'I see,' said Nick slowly. 'You know, I'm beginning to think I've let you in for more than I thought.'

Frankie could not understand his reservations.

'My dear Nick, I'm an adult and quite able to take care of myself.'

'But not a terribly good judge of character, perhaps, Frankie. You're too idealistic. Dive in too quickly. That's why you've been so put off by the toughness of show business. You're not tough, and you're inclined to be a crusader and get knocked about for your pains. You want to play things a bit cooler.'

Frankie surveyed her brother with amused admiration. Nick's air of elegant detachment was splendid armour against the world's pricks, and if his languid manner annoyed some members of the family, it concealed, as she well knew, a needle-sharp mind and more sympathy for human frailty than would ever have been suspected from that calm, handsome face and dilettante appearance. He wore his fair hair rather long, not in modern fashion but with a lock or two flopping over his brow, more in the tradition of the Georgian poets, and he was a fastidious dresser, favouring pastel shirts and wide, gay ties.

'I wish I could play it cooler,' she said, 'but it's no use. I have to have things out. I can't help getting involved.'

'Well, keep me posted. And if you need to be rescued, you know the address for your S.O.S. Now I must be going. I've a book review to get off tonight.'

'Shall I see you at Grandma's monthly bun-fight on Saturday?'

'Bun-fight?' drawled Nick, eyeing his sister severely. 'Are you referring to that ceremonial family gathering which takes place on the first Saturday of every month?'

'I am.'

'Then I'm afraid pressure of work will force me to miss this one.'

'Too bad,' said Frankie. 'I hope you'll sound more convincing when you telephone Grandma.'

'As a matter of fact, the excuse is a genuine one. Although the Rainwoods en masse are a bit much, I usually get a good deal of amusement out of the tribal gatherings, and I enjoy trying to shock Grandma. I never succeed, you know. Age hasn't blunted her mind, and she often has the effrontery to out-quote me, with exquisite courtesy, of course.'

'I shall have to give her a full report of my reasons for quitting the stage and going to Wales,' said Frankie, sighing. 'I don't like this betwixt and between stage. I shall be glad to take the plunge into wild Wales now.'

'Well, remember what I say. Play it cool. Don't plunge. Just dip a toe in and see if the temperature's right. If not, hand in your resignation gracefully. Like to stand me this coffee? Our waitress seems to have disappeared for the night, and I must be off. *Au revoir.*'

He threaded his way through the tables, turned at the door to give her a last salute, and disappeared into the night. When the waitress at last reappeared on the scene, Frankie ordered another coffee, and pondered on the future, not so confident about the new venture as she had appeared to Nick, half excited, half uneasy, about the challenge it presented.

Her reception at Riverdale on that Saturday afternoon was not altogether reassuring, for Caroline Falkland was not there to welcome her, and her absence made a lot of difference. It was Julie who explained.

'Mother's so sorry but she had to go to London yesterday. Grandma's not well. She'll be back on Monday, though, and I'm to show you around.'

In fact, all that Julie did was to help carry Frankie's cases up to her room and tell her that she'd be back later, but she had to slip out to the village. A little bewildered, Frankie looked round the room which was to be her home and drew comfort from its warm charm and the splendour of the view from the window. It was late afternoon, and after a windy, blustery day, the sun was sinking behind the mountains in a sky of fast-moving clouds which reflected its red glow. The area of sky just above the mountains was a gorgeous kaleidoscope of red, crimson, orange, green, blue and purple, with the black outline of the mountains sharp against it. There were only a few streaks of snow on the higher peaks now, but one patch shone like gold as the last rays of the sun moved across it. And then the sun had vanished, and the river valley darkened. It was as she turned from the window that she noticed the small card at the foot of a little bowl of snowdrops on the dressing table.

> Welcome to Riverdale. Please forgive my absence. Unavoidable, alas. I look forward to seeing you on Monday.
> *Caroline.*

Heartened by this, she had a wash and started to unpack. She had nearly finished when a knock at her door heralded Mrs. Filey.

'I've just taken the tea-trolley into the sitting-room,' she said abruptly. 'I've no doubt you can do with a cup of tea after your journey, Miss Barbury.'

'Oh, thank you. I'll be down.'

'Mr. Falkland will see you at dinner. Seven o'clock sharp.'

The door had closed before Frankie could reply. She had tea on her own, half expecting Julie to return, but there was still no sign of her when she went up to her room to change from sweater and skirt into a dress for dinner, a little daunted at the thought of a solitary meal with Mr. Falkland. In fact, she found him quiet and courteous, apologetic for his wife's absence. He ate very little, although the Dover sole was excellently cooked and the crème caramel that followed could not be faulted.

'Rather a poor reception party for you, Miss Barbury,' he said with a faint smile, after Mrs. Filey had brought in the coffee. 'I'm sorry Julie's disappeared, too.'

'That's all right. I'm not quite sure what my duties here will be this weekend.'

'Just look around and settle yourself in, my dear.'

'And then? What sort of routine would you like to arrange, Mr. Falkland? Mrs. Falkland mentioned secretarial duties, and thought you might like me to read to you sometimes and wheel your chair out in the garden. But it was all a little vague.'

'I think she just wants you to be a stand-in for her when she's away or otherwise engaged. I'm a bit of a drag, unfortunately. I think if you come into my study at nine-thirty each weekday morning, I can get you to type any letters necessary. My right hand is useless, and although I've trained myself to do most things left-handed, I find it difficult to write and too much of an effort to type. My eyes get tired easily, too, so if

A Cool Reception

you can spare a little time for reading, I should be grateful. To be deprived of reading in my situation is a sore trial. You have a good voice and with your training should be an excellent reader. Does the idea appeal?'

'Very much.'

'What sort of books do you like?'

'All sorts. Fiction, biographies, classics and light-weight. And plays. Not thrillers or historical novels. I prefer my history plain, and I hate reading about violence.'

'We should fit in very well, then. But two or three hours a day is more than enough for a young girl to spend with a half-paralysed old man. In fact,' he added, his eyes sharp beneath the heavy brows, 'I'll be frank and admit that I don't expect you to stick this job for long. A dismal job for a lively young girl.'

'We'll see. Mrs. Falkland is so gay and charming, and Julie isn't dismal. Life in the country will be a welcome change for me, and I'd like to be of use to you,' she added, moved by that ravaged figured face in some strange way which she could not analyse, for his manner was often disconcerting and did not invite sympathy.

'We'll see,' he said, echoing her. 'Now, my dear, if you'll excuse me, I've some papers to sort out for my son. He's looking in shortly. No, I can manipulate this chair all right on a level surface, thank you. If you would just open this door and my study door for me. Did Julie say where she was going tonight?'

'No. In fact, I gathered that she was only going to slip out to the village before the shops shut and I expected her back. But perhaps I was mistaken.'

He shook his head, frowning.

'Julie's given too free a rein. Never know where she is. I'd be grateful if you would keep an eye on her, Miss Barbury. I, as you realise, am in no position to do so, and her mother discourages her from . . . troubling me. Too much so, I'm afraid.'

'I'll do my best. Seventeen is a difficult age.'

'When guidance is very important. Julie gets none,' he said abruptly, then as though regretting saying as much, inclined his head and manipulated his chair through the sitting-room door, across the hall and into his study.

'Goodnight, Miss Barbury,' he said. 'If you need anything, ask Mrs. Filey.'

And once again, Frankie was on her own. Feeling a little at a loss, she made up the fire in the sitting-room, and was glancing through a pile of magazines on the window seat when a voice behind her startled her and made her spin round to see Rolf Falkland.

'Good evening, Miss Barbury. I forgot you were due to arrive today.'

'Good evening.'

'I'm sorry if I startled you.'

'I didn't hear you arrive.'

'I have my own key.'

'You tread lightly.'

'The carpets are thick. Is my stepmother around?'

'No. She's in London until Monday.'

'So. She's quickly availing herself of your services.'

'That,' said Frankie gently, 'is what the job's about.'

'Quite. And Julie?'

'Out. I don't know where.'

He was looking at her through narrowed eyes, then his expression seemed to become a shade less wintry as he said, 'At least my father is at home.'

'Yes. He's expecting you.'

He lit a cigarette, and there was an unnerving silence between them for a few moments. Then he said quietly, 'My father is a very sick man, Miss Barbury. It's essential that he shouldn't be worried or disturbed. The condition of his heart is poor. If, when you're on your own here, as you're likely to be quite a lot, anything crops up which you feel you can't cope with yourself, ring me. I can get here in ten minutes if necessary. My father's peace of mind must be guarded at all costs.'

'I'll remember.'

'My telephone number is in the book by the telephone in the hall. I may be the last person you would wish to turn to. We seem to have got off on the wrong foot. But it's my father we must think of.'

'I'll see that as far as it's in my power he isn't worried.'

'Thank you.'

He nodded and left her. He moved with a lithe grace, light on his feet for such a tall man. No wonder she hadn't heard him. There was a strange, alien quality about him. Not timid by nature, she was disconcerted to find herself a little afraid of him. But his concern for his father was genuine, indicating some small streak of humanity there.

Julie did not return until nearly half past ten.

'I met a friend in the village,' she said airily.

'I thought you'd only slipped out for a short time. You father asked me where you were, but I'd no idea.'

'With a friend. He knows I'm never in to dinner when Caro's away. I can't bear those silent meals with him. Is Rolf with him? I heard voices in the study.'

'Yes.'

'I'm off to bed. There's nothing you want?' she added as an afterthought, pausing at the door.

'Nothing, thank you,' said Frankie calmly.

The milk of human kindness seemed a little thin in that member of the family, also. Her father was right. She needed guidance. But at seventeen, it was rather late.

4

Cross Threads

WITH Caroline's return, Frankie found herself slotted into a pleasant enough routine. She was at Mr. Falkland's disposal for the first part of the morning, then at Caroline's for any odd commissions to the village or the little market town of Mynelly three miles away. The afternoon was her own until five o'clock, when she spent an hour or two reading to Mr. Falkland or learning to play chess, at which he was highly skilled.

'A splendid exercise for the brain, my dear. Keeps mine from growing rusty from disuse.'

She was free again after dinner, and was always happy to spend this time with Caroline, whose charm in no way diminished with familiarity, but whose visits to her mother became more frequent. With Julie, Frankie found herself rather at a loss. The girl was pleasant enough, but somehow withheld her confidence and was oddly elusive. Frankie talked to Caroline about this one evening in March, when they were sitting by the fire.

'I know you wanted me to be a companion for Julie, and I'd like to be, but I can't honestly say I've made much progress.'

'Well, at that age, you know, children are rather self-absorbed. You're doing all, and more, than I expected, Frankie, and there's absolutely no need to worry about Julie. I believe in giving children freedom.'

'Well, you're her ideal. I can't expect to compete,' said Frankie, smiling. 'She's aching for you to take her with you to London.'

'I daresay, but school has first claim on her time, and I feel that an invalid father is depressing enough without inflicting an invalid grandmother on the child. Sickness can have a morbid effect on adolescents. I shall have to go up to Mother's again on Friday. She sounded very low when I phoned her last night. I'd hoped to have a quiet weekend, too.'

'You need it,' said Frankie. 'Those trips tire you.'

'I know. How I envy those strong robust types like Trevor's relations! Or Mrs. Filey. Absolutely untiring.'

'You should let me do more,' said Frankie, for Caroline looked fragile enough to be shattered by a puff of wind, and always spent some hours of every day lying on the couch either in her own room or the sitting-room.

'But you do so much, Frankie. How I did without you, I can't imagine. Anyway, it's an ill wind that blows no good, because having to go to London next weekend will at least spare me the burden of the Falkland family party on Saturday. Naughty of me, and they're really good-hearted people, but I've never felt that they accepted me, that I fit in.'

'Are they celebrating anything special?'

'Yes. Elwyn's birthday. My brother-in-law. I don't think I'd want to celebrate my fifty-sixth birthday, but Elwyn loves a party and seizes on any excuse. The trouble is, Trevor will insist on going, and he really isn't up to it. Getting him in and out of Rolf's car tires him, for a start. But he says he must make the effort.'

'Well, I can understand that. He must feel rather cut off, and want to keep up what family contacts he can.'

'Yes, of course. Just because they don't really take me to their hearts is no reason for discouraging Trevor. There's nothing I like better than to find ways of relieving his solitude, poor darling. It's just that I worry about the extra strain. But Welsh people are very clannish. That's why I don't fit, perhaps. A Londoner, me. I'm sure they think that when Trevor married again, he should have chosen a Welsh woman nearer his own age.'

'They must be very wrong-headed, then, if they still think like that,' said Frankie, for Caroline, with her pretty face and charming ways, must surely lighten her husband's dim life.

'Nice Frankie,' said Caroline, smiling, her head on one side. 'But I mustn't be unfair to the family. Inevitable that they should have a narrow outlook, living such parochial lives. Hullo, darling,' she added as Julie came in. 'Had a nice evening?'

'Mmm. Josie had some new pop records,' said Julie, throwing her coat over a chair and coming to the fire.

'You're losing a lot of beauty sleep these days,' said her mother shaking her head.

'Can I come up to London with you next time you go, Caro? I want a special dress for a dance, and I'd love to go round the London shops.'

'Not next time, darling. I'm going this weekend, and I shall be tied up with Grandma. But I'll see if we can arrange something in your Easter holidays. Just the two of us,' she said, smiling at her daughter's sulky face.

'You always put me off. Why not this weekend? I can go off on my own if you can't leave Grandma.'

'One, I don't want you to miss two days from school. Two, you're going to Uncle Elwyn's birthday party on Saturday.'

Julie wrinkled her nose.

'I don't mind missing that. Are you going?' she asked Frankie.

'Me? Well, no. I haven't been asked. I don't know them.'

'You've been asked. I saw the letter.'

Frankie turned to Caroline questioningly, but Caroline herself looked as surprised as Frankie as she said, 'Has she? I must confess I didn't take much notice of the letter. I just glanced at it and passed it over to your father. But I doubt whether Frankie wants to get involved there. Julie, will you be an angel and make a jug of your special coffee? Shocking to drink coffee last thing at night, I know, but I have an addiction to it, and your coffee is so much better than Mrs. Filey's.'

Julie went. Caroline began to talk about a new play that had just made a hit in London, and from there went on to question Frankie about her acting experiences. When Julie returned with the coffee, Caroline dominated the conversation with a vivacious description of her own early experiences on the stage. Then, suddenly wilting, she bade them both an affectionate goodnight and left them. Julie followed her almost at once, and Frankie was left to take the tray of coffee cups out to the kitchen without once having had the opportunity of reverting to the invitation. She didn't like coffee at this late hour, either, and didn't know why she had accepted it. Somehow, one followed Caroline's lead.

It was Trevor Falkland who brought up the question of the invitation the next morning.

'I'm glad you'll have a chance to get to know the family on Saturday,' he said, after she had typed two letters for him.

'I only learned that I was included in the invitation last night.'

'But you're coming?' he queried sharply.

Frankie hesitated. The words which had remained unspoken last night had nevertheless made it clear that Caroline was not in favour, but she could hardly mention this.

'You've another engagement?' he said as Frankie remained silent.

'Oh no. But I'm a stranger to them and . . .'

'All the more reason for you to go and get acquainted. This is a lonely life for a young girl. My nephew and niece are nice young people, and it'll be good for you to meet them. You go and enjoy yourself, my dear.'

'Thank you. I will.'

But she mentioned it to Caroline later that day.

'Will you mind?' she asked, for she was not good at dressing things up.

Caroline's blue-grey eyes opened wide.

'Dear Frankie, of course not, if you wish to go. I can trust you to stay in my camp, I know.' She hesitated, then added gently, 'It makes me unhappy, this rift between me and the family, and I've tried to mend it, but when all my efforts are undone by one who's implacably hostile, the best I can do is try to ignore it.'

'And that one is?'

'Rolf. I shouldn't tell you if you weren't going to get involved with them, because I hate talking about people like this, but perhaps you should be fore-warned. And I'd be sad if they tried to turn you against me. We're such good friends.'

'You don't have to worry on that score. I know my own mind, and hostilities have already broken out between me and Rolf. He seems so suspicious. I can't imagine why.'

'Just because I employ you and we're good friends would be reason enough. I have to confess that I've failed utterly with Rolf, but I can truthfully say that I've tried my utmost to win his affection. He was thirteen years old when his father married me, and from the word go, he resented me. I try not to judge too harshly. It's hard for a child to adjust to a new mother, and I think a lot of the blame can be attributed to that Spanish grandmother of his who stepped in when Rolf's mother died and looked after the boy.'

'How old was Rolf when his mother died?'

'Nine. Old Mrs. Albyon had him under her care for four years. What he was like before that, I don't know. But the old lady hated me, and I'm sure it was her influence that made it impossible for me to gain Rolf's affection. She was a wicked old woman. I can see her black glittering eyes now. Rolf has the same eyes.'

'I thought there was some foreign element in his appearance when I first saw him. He's half Spanish, then?'

'No. His mother's father was English. So Rolf's a mixture of Spanish, English and Welsh. A mongrel. And a dangerous mixture, too. Small wonder that my ingenuous efforts to win his affection went for nothing.'

'He seems very attached to his father.'

'Well . . . perhaps. There are material reasons why he should be so. Rolf's is not an affectionate nature. But I still have hopes for him. He's become friendly with a rich Canadian girl who's over here on a year's vacation, staying at a hotel near Mynelly owned by her uncle. She's helping in the reception. A nice, sensible young woman. She might do much for Rolf. And what's more, her father's in the same line of business as the Falklands—building contractors, but on a worldwide scale, with headquarters in Canada. It would be a splendid opportunity for Rolf. To do him justice, he's very able. Trained to be an architect and surveyor. He originally intended to go into practice on his own, but in the end he joined the family business. He'd have much more scope for his talents in Canada with the Heston organisation, though. So, on all counts, I'd be happy to see him marry Tracey.'

'He might perhaps not want to go abroad and leave his father at this stage.'

'Trevor wouldn't wish to stand in his way. He has me to look after him. But, of course, Rolf distrusts me. Anyway, I keep hoping. Nobody really knows what goes on in Rolf's mind. I wonder if you'd put another log on the fire, dear. I don't seem able to get warm tonight. I wish I could persuade Trevor to go abroad for the winter. This Welsh climate's so dreary. But he won't.'

'Well, it's nearly spring now,' said Frankie, making up the fire.

'It doesn't feel like it,' said Caroline, shivering and putting a cushion over her feet at the end of the sofa before picking up a magazine.

'I'd better be off to my chess instruction. I'm afraid I'm not making very rapid progress,' said Frankie ruefully.

Caroline smiled.

'Dear Frankie. You're so patient with Trevor.'

'Not at all. He's patient with me.'

But that evening, Trevor Falkland was not in the mood for chess. He seemed more tired than usual and dispirited.

'Read me some verse, Miss Barbury,' he said, for he had not yet lapsed into the familiarity of her Christian name, as had everybody else, even Rolf, and treated her always with old-fashioned courtesy. '*Intimations of Immortality*. I'm in need of some philosophy to comfort me this evening. And your husky little voice is a comfort in itself.'

It was rare for him to make personal remarks, and she smiled her appreciation as she took the volume of Wordsworth from the bookshelf and began to read. When she had finished, there was silence for a few moments, until he said, 'Thank you, my dear. A wonderful poem. I'm not sure that the brave ending makes up for the stabs on the way, though.

> Whither is fled the visionary gleam?
> Where is it now, the glory and the dream?

That stab goes too deep for healing.'

Frankie was moved, as so often, by the sad, ravaged face of the crippled man. She wished she did not feel so helpless to alleviate things for him, but he locked his thoughts away and his reserve put an unbridgeable chasm between them. She wondered what Nick would make of him. She had from the first realised that she would never learn anything of the past from Trevor Falkland, and any idea of seeking an introduction for Nick had been scotched at birth.

'It's going to be a lovely sunset,' she said. 'I'll draw the curtains back so that you can see more of it.'

After a cold day of racing clouds, the sky had cleared and the sun was casting a warm glow over the mountains as it sank.

'And you should be out, enjoying it. Not wasting your youth indoors with a cripple. Run along, my dear, and leave me to reconcile my thoughts with Wordsworth's conclusions. No arguing. Remember:

> Nothing can bring back the hour
> Of splendour in the grass, of glory in the flower.

That hour is yours now. I wouldn't rob you of a minute of it. Make the most of it. Wales is a beautiful country. Go out and get to know it.'

'But I have plenty of time to do that.'

'There is never plenty of time. This particular evening in March, when the smell of spring is in the air and the sun is going down behind the mountains in a clear sky, is unique and not to be missed. You have seeing eyes for that splendour and that glory. Go out and use them.'

He had wheeled his chair to the window to watch the sky,

and she laid a hand on his shoulder in an impulsive little gesture of thanks. He patted it, then said abruptly, 'Before you go, tell Mrs. Filey I'll have dinner in here tonight.'

She left him alone by the window, feeling that they had made that chasm between them a little narrower that evening.

It was true that she was finding great happiness in the wild beauty of the countryside round Riverdale after the confines of London, and Trevor Falkland had told her of several walks which she might not have discovered for herself. His intimate knowledge of the countryside, too, made her realise how cruelly he must feel his confinement.

That evening, she took the path away from the river through a coppice where a few days before she had found wild daffodils in bloom. She sought the small clearing again and the sight of those bright flowers swaying in the wild gladdened her heart and reminded her of Wordsworth again. It was odd how the most hackneyed lines sprang to life with moving truth and beauty when the experience they described was shared. The sinking sun cast a flickering pattern of light and shade in the coppice, where hazel catkins swung gold, and the white flowers of wood anemones danced on their slender stems. A blackbird rushed by her with wisps of dead grass bunched in its beak, and was lost to sight before she could trace the nest. Spring, with all its promise of hope and renewal, was pushing winter aside.

As she emerged from the coppice, the sun dipped behind the mountain, and immediately the valley felt cold. She stepped out briskly across the meadow and back to the riverside path. Here, the water ran swiftly over a shallow boulder-strewn bed between banks of tall grass and ferns until it broadened out and became more peaceful as she neared Riverdale, and darkened by overhanging birch and alder trees.

She had stopped to retie her shoe-lace when a high-pitched giggling distracted her. It seemed to come from somewhere ahead of her. Rounding the bend, she saw a slender girl and a thick-set man in a close embrace. In the half-light, the girl's fair hair showed up palely against the dark material of her coat. The man seemed to be making a thorough business of it until the girl pushed him off, giggling again, and with his arm round her shoulders walked slowly round the next bend. Frankie came out into the lane in time to see a white car drive off, leaving the girl looking after it. If she had turned, she must have seen Frankie, but she walked quickly towards Riverdale.

She was about a hundred yards ahead and the gathering darkness soon hid her from sight.

So that was why Julie was so elusive. The man had given Frankie the impression of being much older than Julie, and she could not help feeling a little uneasy, remembering the late hours Julie kept and the vague explanations. Caroline gave her complete freedom, and never seemed curious about her long absences. Only her father voiced misgivings sometimes, but he saw little of her. She seemed afraid of him, and Frankie felt that Caroline did nothing to dispel this fear, keeping Julie away from him as much as possible, probably to spare him any worry, but Frankie thought he might welcome a chance to get to know his daughter better.

Almost unnoticed, a few threads of uneasiness were weaving themselves into the pleasant pattern of her life at Riverdale. Nothing specific. Just a vague feeling that the picture wasn't quite right. A mongrel. Caroline had enunciated those two words in a tone Frankie had never heard from her before. She always spoke so softly and gently and with such good nature, making excuses for people when she could not praise them. But Rolf would try the tolerance of an angel, and she was sure that Caroline had suffered a lot at his hands over the years. That she remained so gay and kind in the face of her stepson's enmity, her husband's state of health and her own fragility was a tribute to her courage. Any criticism of her by the Falklands in Frankie's presence would receive short shrift. If they were all as hard and suspicious as Rolf, Caroline certainly needed an ally, and she had one. She would welcome the opportunity of taking up arms on her behalf against Rolf. Then she had to smile at herself ruefully. She could hear Nick's cool voice saying, 'Another crusade, Frankie?'

5
Two Camps

WHEN the time came, Trevor Falkland felt unable to make the effort to go to his brother's party.

'I've spoken to Rolf. He's coming to fetch you and Julie. Perhaps you'd give these cigars to Elwyn, with my best wishes. Sorry to miss the party, but I guess I'm no asset, and to get me in and out of a car and transport my wheel-chair, too, presents as many difficulties as transporting an elephant. Just don't feel up to it today.'

'Then I shall stay here, too, as Caroline's away.'

'Nonsense. Quite unnecessary. Mrs. Filey's at hand. She and I are used to each other.'

'But I feel it's my job to be here.'

'My dear, Mrs. Filey has had the doubtful satisfaction of having me in her sole charge for more times than I care to remember. Whole weeks when my wife and Julie have gone off on holiday. Mrs. Filey's an extremely capable woman, and I'm not entirely helpless. You and Julie must go along and enjoy yourselves. That's final,' he concluded, and there was no arguing with that.

At the last minute, Julie cried off, too. She said she had a bad headache and was going to bed.

'Why not take a couple of aspirins and chance it? You may feel better in half an hour,' said Frankie.

'No. Family parties bore me, anyway. Likely to make a headache worse. Caro said I could please myself about whether I went. I'm not going to make a martyr of myself and go with a headache.'

And so Frankie went alone to meet the people whom she had first seen in the hotel, feeling rather like a lone fighter in the enemy camp.

'I'm sorry you've had the trouble of coming out here just to fetch me,' she said to Rolf. 'If I'd known earlier that neither

Julie nor your father were going, I could have hired the man from the village.'

'Oh, I think you'll find me as safe a driver as Jim Davis,' said Rolf imperturbably. 'In any case, I wanted to see my father. Shall we go?'

Sitting beside him in his long grey car, she could find nothing to say. She always felt uncomfortable with him. A legacy of his early suspicions of her, although when they met at Riverdale now, he was pleasant enough. Their meetings were brief, though. He spent all his time there with his father.

'The old man's poorly,' he said as they nosed their way through the narrow lanes.

'Yes. I'm so sorry for him. He's very stoical and hates to be a burden. That must be the worst of it. To be dependent.'

'Yes. As a family, we don't take kindly to dependence on others, either. Imprisonment bears hardly on my father, but you're making it a good deal pleasanter for him, he tells me. For that, he's grateful. And so am I.'

Braced for hostility as she was, he had taken the wind out of her sails.

'I enjoy what little I'm able to do for him. We get on very well together. My only handicap is my slow grasp of chess,' she added lightly.

'Not a game for the young and lively. Anyway, with such a delectable voice and acting ability as yours, I gather he's taking great delight in going through all of Shakespeare again, and chess is falling into the background.'

'Well, I'm better at reading plays than I am at chess. That's certain.'

'Do you miss it? The stage, I mean.'

'Not really. But then I was out of work so much. I regret not making the grade, just because nobody likes a sense of failure, but I found it a disillusioning profession in more ways than one. I don't think I was really cut out for it.'

'And you like your job here?'

'Yes. Caroline is a delightful employer. Although employer seems the wrong word. We're good friends. Nobody could fail to like her.'

'She has great charm,' said Rolf drily.

'And is so good-hearted. She's tiring herself out trying to look after her mother from this distance. She's really not at all strong herself.'

'Well, let's hope that you find the rest of the family as agreeable. Your first inspection of them seemed pretty thorough, but first impressions aren't always reliable,' he said with the smooth urbanity he used with such deadly effect.

'In my case, I've always found them pretty reliable.'

'Your judgment is to be envied then,' he replied gravely. 'I've always found people a good deal more complex than that.'

'And you view them with suspicion?'

'Shall we say, caution?'

She glanced at him quickly. She had a feeling that he was laughing at her, but in the dim light of the car his profile revealed nothing of his feelings.

'I'm not cautious enough, am I?'

He smiled, then, and said, 'No, Frankie, you're not. If those first impressions hadn't already told you, somebody else has, that I'm a foxy character. That being so, you should cover up better when boxing with me. And no matter how black my character, I assure you that the rest of the Falklands are quite decent and harmless, so put your fists down.'

They were running through the little market town of Mynelly and before Frankie could find any words to rebuff this man who seemed to read her mind so easily, he had drawn up outside a large, square house a short distance along the lane leading from the town.

And, in fact, Frankie did find the Falklands disarmingly kind, and to her surprise thoroughly enjoyed herself from the moment when the dark-haired, middle-aged woman who was Elwyn's wife, Gwendolyn, welcomed her.

'We're delighted to have the chance of getting to know you,' she said with a warm smile as she took Frankie's coat. 'We've heard how much you are doing for poor Trevor, and Caroline has been singing your praises without letting us get a glimpse of you. Now we must make up for lost time.'

The party she had seen at the hotel sorted itself out as she was introduced. Elwyn was the round, jolly man, who accepted his brother's gift of cigars and Frankie's good wishes with a beaming smile and twinkling blue eyes. His bald pate shone as though it had been polished and his fifty-six years seemed to weigh lightly on him. The sandy-haired young man, Barry, was his son, and the brown-haired girl who had sat next to Rolf at the hotel dinner-party was Deborah, his daughter. The pugnacious man turned out to be Lloyd, the third Falkland brother. Another middle-aged couple, who were old friends and neighbours, a red-headed young man called Evan, and Tracey Heston completed the party.

Two Camps 39

Frankie, curious to see what manner of woman pleased that hard, seemingly inhuman man, Rolf, and what manner of woman it was who could bear with his arrogance, eyed Tracey with some interest when the opportunity presented itself. She was a tall young woman, in her late twenties Frankie guessed, with red hair, good grey eyes and a rather voluptuous look which went oddly with her frank, down-to-earth manner. She appeared well able to look after herself, and she and Rolf were on easy, bantering terms. Her Canadian voice was a little hard, but the general impression was effective and pleasing.

It was a lively, argumentative party, and Frankie soon found that Welsh people were nothing if not fluent and volatile. Accustomed as she had become over the past weeks to a quiet, comparatively solitary life, she found it at first a little bewildering, then stimulating.

'You'll think us a wild lot, Frankie,' said Deborah Falkland, joining her while the rest of the party were embroiled in a heated discussion of the merits of an international rugby club. Evan, up in arms at the suggestion that his hero had given away a try and lost the game for his side on the previous Saturday, appeared to have most of the Falkland family against him.

'Very lively. I'm enjoying it and taking no sides.'

'How do you like our country? Isn't it beautiful?'

'I wouldn't dare say otherwise,' said Frankie gravely, and elicited a smile from Deborah. 'But, in fact, I do think it's beautiful, and I'm looking forward to better weather to explore it.'

'This must be a great change from London. You miss your friends, I expect.'

'London's not all that good for making friends. And I'm used to travelling round a bit.'

'My world's a very small one. I don't think I could bear to go away from my friends and the family. But in a village community it's different, I suppose. You all seem to belong, somehow. And I'm not a very enterprising person, anyway. I wish I were.'

'Why? You're happy being what you are. If enterprising means having a go at all sorts of things, I suppose I might be called enterprising, but I've got nowhere.'

'I can't believe that. And anybody who can be a companion to Uncle Trevor and earn his praise must be very clever. He has a brilliant brain. The only intellectual one of the family, except perhaps for Rolf. I feel so sorry for Uncle Trevor and

I've tried to get under his reserve and cheer him up, but of course I've no adequate mental equipment for the job. I'm better with sick animals.'

'Is that your job?'

'Yes. I work for the local vet. Only an assistant. But I love the work.'

'That's all that matters, then,' said Frankie, who liked this soft-voiced girl with the dark brown eyes and gentle manner. She had underestimated her age when she had seen her at the hotel. She guessed her now to be about twenty. A very unsophisticated twenty.

She encouraged her to talk about her job until Barry came up and said breezily, 'Come along, girls. Break it up. Not the time for female confidences. It's supper time and you might spare a thought for the males.'

'They've all been absorbed in that utterly boring subject of rugby football. We're the neglected ones,' said Deborah.

'Boring? Rugby? And you of Welsh blood. Shame on you, Debbie. Come along, Frankie. Sit next to me at supper and tell me all about the scandals of the theatre. And all that permissiveness of swinging London. Our minds need broadening down here.'

She sat between Barry and Evan, and with the table laden with good food, presenting a choice of cold salmon, game pie, chicken and ham, followed by an array of trifle, apple pie, fruit flans and bowls of strawberries and cream, to say nothing of the Stilton and Cheddar cheese, it was surprising that the party's volubility seemed in no way to diminish, although the food did. Only Rolf seemed a little apart. Cool, detached, incisive, he said less than the others, but counted for more when he did join in. His looks set him apart from the others, too. The male Falklands were of stocky build, whereas Rolf was tall with some of the lean elegance she had noticed in Spanish dancers. A kind of whipcord strength. And the high bridged nose, gleaming black eyes and high forehead suggested that the Spanish blood in him contributed more to his appearance than either the English or Welsh.

They drank to Elwyn's health, he responded genially and proposed a toast to absent friends, in particular Trevor. And then they were off again on a passionate discussion of the Welsh nationalist movement. With feelings running high, Frankie found her eyes meeting Rolf's across the table, and he raised his eyebrows and gave her a quirky little smile, as though they were both onlookers on the touch-line where this particular battle was concerned. She found that silent little exchange surprisingly warming.

Afterwards, the younger members of the party danced in the large square hall while the others still carried on the argument over coffee in the sitting-room. Barry led off with Frankie, Evan paired off with Deborah, and Rolf with Tracey. Frankie, a neat, nimble dancer, fitted in well with the rumbustious Barry, who liked to improvise. When Rolf asked her for the next dance, and drew her closely to him, it was another style altogether. Not for him the flinging apart and gyrating and wriggling which Barry favoured. Graceful, rhythmical, perfectly balanced, they moved as one, although for it to be absolutely perfect, Frankie considered that she needed an extra few inches in height to match him. Those few inches Tracey had, but she looked to be a little heavy on her feet, thought Frankie watching them later. She could detect no particular air of intimacy between them, and Tracey seemed just as friendly with Evan and Barry as with Rolf. Not that Rolf would ever betray his feelings to others. He remained an enigma. Of his strong physical attraction, however, there was no doubt, and the underlining of this fact when he danced with her again set little warning bells ringing in her mind, reminding her that this man was dangerous.

She had kept in mind Caroline's warning about being drawn into the enemy camp, but on the one or two occasions when Caroline's name had been mentioned, there had been no suggestion of criticism, and, with the exception of Rolf, she could not think these Falklands ill-natured people or dissemblers. In fact, their feelings came tumbling out about everybody and everything with the most fluent frankness. Rolf was a different matter. He kept his cards to himself, and his poker-faced manner with Caroline supported her contention that he was hostile. It was that same cool hostility which had chilled Frankie on that first night at the hotel, and in the early days of her employment at Riverdale. Just lately, though, she felt that his attitude to her was changing. A friendlier warmth seemed to be seeping through his armour, but she was still not sure enough of him to trust this, and remained on her guard.

It was for this reason that she parried him that night when, driving her back to Riverdale, he touched again on that first encounter.

'Well, Frankie, do they improve on acquaintance?' he asked.

'I like them all very much. But then I never did disapprove of them.'

'No? The searching examination we were submitted to at the hotel that night would have done justice to a detective keeping his eye on a gang of pickpockets. At least, that's what seemed to be coming my way.'

'Just idle curiosity. And you reminded me of a producer of a play who'd given me a very hard time. In fact, I think it was he who finally demolished my hopes of an acting career.'

'And you really had no idea who we were, although you were going to apply for the job with my stepmother the next day?'

'No idea at all. And when you talk of a detective trailing pickpockets, aren't you describing your attitude rather than mine? The look you gave me was condemnation without trial, and you kept it up, too. What about that grilling you gave me when you took me back to the hotel after I'd seen Caroline?' demanded Frankie, who believed in attack as the best means of defence.

'I'll admit to suspicions which I now think were unfounded. I apologise. But I had reasons.' He hesitated. 'My father is in a very vulnerable position, Frankie. I have to protect him.'

'From what? He's well looked after. Caroline's always most concerned that he shouldn't be worried in any way. And I do my best, too. I like and admire him so much.'

'Yes. I'm more than relieved about that.'

'But why should you ever have suspected that I might be a threat to your father, for heaven's sake? It sounds crazy.'

'Yes. I realise it must do, but there are circumstances I can't discuss with you. Things you don't know, and are too young and guileless to understand, perhaps.'

'Well, can I take it that I am no longer suspected of criminal intent?' she asked lightly, not much liking his term guileless. It had a connotation of childish foolishness.

'Answer me two questions first. Then I'll answer yours.'

'Two to one. But I've nothing to hide, Inspector. Carry on.'

'Do you have any connection with a newspaper or magazine? I ask because my father was being pestered for an interview just before you came. I thought it possible that you might be a journalist sent to find out by devious methods what couldn't be obtained by a straightforward interview. The press doesn't give up that easily.'

And right out of the blue, he had lobbed a hot chestnut into her lap. She had promised Caroline to say nothing of her connection with Nick. She had taken the job in all faith for its own sake, and although Trevor Falkland's past intrigued her in view of Nick's information, she could honestly say that prying into it was no part of her plan. Her impulse then was to tell him, but if she did so, he might make trouble, tell his father, and refuse to believe that she was not acting for Nick. She might lose her job, upset Caroline and leave her employer with the whole burden of Riverdale on her fragile shoulders once more. With Caroline's appeal to her not to join the enemy camp still in her ears, she hesitated. A little more trust in him, and she would have told him. But Caroline won, and she said firmly, 'I'm no journalist. It all sounds far-fetched to me. What has your father to fear? He dislikes publicity. Refuses an interview. Surely that's all there is to it.'

'People are apt to get phobias as they grow old. My father has feared the press ever since a personal tragedy when he was quite young showed them at their worst. His state of health now is such that at all costs he mustn't get worked up.'

He spoke abstractedly, as though something in her reply had bothered him, and she felt uneasy, wishing that circumstances had not placed her in this ambiguous position with a man to whom ambiguity was unacceptable. If ever a man had 'no compromise' stamped on him, that man was Rolf Falkland. But although in actual fact she did have some second-hand contact with a journalist and thus might be considered a party to what he had suspected, in intent she was innocent. And that was all that mattered. Comforted by this, she said, 'That's your first question answered. The second?'

'Did you know Caroline in London before you came here?'

Surprised, she said, 'No. The first time I saw her was at the hotel that night. What makes you think I might have known her before?'

'Oh, it was all fixed up so quickly and easily. Your coming here, I mean. No references. No hesitation on either side, it seemed.'

'Perhaps Caroline, like me, relies on first impressions.'

They had left Mynelly behind and were nearly back to Riverdale. He still seemed thoughtful, and after a few moments of silence, she said, 'You haven't answered my question. I've answered yours. Am I still a suspect?'

'You're a woman, and therefore always suspect,' he said a little wryly.

'You said I was young and guileless just now.'

'Point to you.'

He stopped the car just short of the gates of Riverdale and switched on the interior lights of the car. When he turned to her, she felt herself trembling. He took her face between his hands and scrutinised it with a grave intensity that seemed to bore into her so that she felt utterly defenceless, as though he knew all that was in her mind.

'You have very beautiful eyes, Frankie. The colour of the Aegean sea. I think they're honest eyes.'

Then he released her, saying gently, 'Goodnight. I'm glad you came to the party. I'll leave you to walk up the drive, as it's a fine night.'

'Of course,' she said a little breathlessly. 'But isn't it easier for you to turn the car round in front of the house?'

'There's something about my stepmother's home that chills me as soon as I drive through the gates. You see, I have my phobias, too. And I'd rather end the evening on this pleasant, warm note.'

Walking up the drive on that cold, clear night, Frankie felt confused and shaken. Friend? Enemy? He was just as great an enigma. But in his arms, dancing, the questions of her mind had been blown aside like chaff in the wind. And with his hands cupping her cheeks in a moment of tense intimacy, they hadn't seemed to matter at all. Now they buzzed again in her head like troublesome bees. Had she convinced him? Why all this fuss about publicity? Could she trust him, or was he somehow trying to get at Caroline through her? And why must there be two camps, anyway?

Preoccupied, she let herself in, to be met in the hall by Mrs. Filey, clad in a red dressing-gown, her hair in a grey pigtail. She seemed surprised to see Frankie.

'I thought you were in, Miss Barbury. I heard someone go upstairs ten minutes ago.'

'You must have been mistaken, Mrs. Filey. Unless Mrs. Falkland has returned sooner than expected.'

'There's no train from London arriving this hour. And I was not mistaken. That's why I came downstairs to turn the hall light off. I could see it shining out across the lawn, and thought you'd forgotten to turn it off. I don't doubt it was Miss Julie.'

'But she went to bed with a headache.'

'It obviously got better,' said Mrs. Filey grimly. 'I'll say goodnight, then, and leave you to switch off the light.'

'Goodnight,' said Frankie.

She was remembering that as Rolf had turned into the lane, a car was moving ahead of them, beyond Riverdale, picking up speed. A white car.

6
The Forsaken Garden

SHE tackled Julie about it the next morning.

'You went out last night, then, after all, Julie?'

Julie looked disconcerted for a moment, then said airily, 'What makes you say that?'

'I saw the back of your friend's car when I came back, and Mrs. Filey mentioned that you'd come in ten minutes before. At least, she'd assumed it was me and then met me in the hall when she came down to turn off the light.'

'Old nosy-parker.'

'Not at all. She didn't seem particularly interested. But I am. You knew you were going out when you pleaded a headache. Why lie about it?'

'Why not? Little white lies do no harm and save a lot of fuss. I had a more attractive invitation, that's all.'

'Wasn't that discourteous to your relatives, since you'd already accepted their invitation, to say nothing of the fact of lying to me and your father.'

Julie shrugged her shoulders.

'I've told you. It was just to save a fuss. My father mustn't be annoyed. Caro wouldn't have minded a bit. She's not keen on my fraternising with the Falklands, anyway.'

'She might like to know who you are out with, though.'

Julie's grey-blue eyes, so like her mother's, studied Frankie for a moment, then she gave her a little smile which seemed to indicate that Frankie didn't know what she was talking about, and said 'Caro wouldn't mind. She never interferes. You can tell her if you like.'

'Who is this friend, then? Why not bring him home?'

'To this miserable house? It's only bearable when Caro's here, and she's often tired and not all that interested. We go our own ways here. I should have thought you'd have realised that by now.'

It was hard to believe just then that Julie was a schoolgirl;

The Forsaken Garden

she spoke with a cynicism that shocked Frankie. But there was something about the girl which made her feel sorry for her, too, and she spoke gently.

'I'm interested, though, Julie. Who is your friend? Can't you tell me something about him?'

'I'll introduce you to him some time, perhaps,' she said coolly, 'but I'm due to meet him at ten this morning, so if you'll excuse me. I've told Mrs. Filey that I shan't be here for any meals today. So long.'

Troubled, Frankie saw her running down the drive a few minutes later. She was wearing an emerald green suit, with black patent shoes and handbag. Her fair hair hung smoothly to her shoulders. Nothing about her suggested a schoolgirl. She was seventeen, but might have passed for twenty-seven. From her glimpse of the man, Frankie was sure that he was a good deal older than Julie, and, judging from the car, fairly well endowed with this world's goods.

Was she worrying unnecessarily? She had always been given a lot of freedom herself, to an extent frowned upon by her grandmother, but the family had always been there to turn to, and its standards had always been a guide-line to her, to say nothing of the close interest which Mirabel Rainwood maintained in her grandchildren, and the influence which she exerted by her own example of self-discipline. But Julie had no guide-lines, it seemed. She shunned her father, half scared of him. Caroline indulged her, and in any case was away from home a good deal. She sighed. The longer she knew this family, the more complex it became. Their relationships had all seemed so straightforward at first. Now secrets and lies and baffling undercurrents which she could sense but not chart created a state of affairs where she felt she must move warily, where things were not what they seemed. She would be glad when Caroline was back. It always seemed brighter then.

At the first opportunity, sure that Caroline would be concerned in spite of Julie's assurances to the contrary, Frankie brought up the subject of Julie's involvement with this stranger and her truancy the previous Saturday.

'Naughty girl,' said Caroline, but she was smiling. 'I have to confess, though, that I'd probably have done the same myself at her age.'

'But don't you want to know what sort of person he is? Julie's only seventeen, after all, and he appeared to be a lot older.'

'Why Frankie, you're only twenty-one yourself; you can't

have forgotten what these adolescent crushes are like. And Julie's got a good head on her shoulders, you know.'

'Yes, perhaps I'm making a fuss about nothing. It's just that Julie is still at school, and hasn't any experience yet of the adult world. Men can take advantage of that.'

'It's sweet of you to care. I'll have a word with her about this mysterious Don Juan. But I believe in showing children that you trust them. In giving them responsibility for themselves.'

But you have a responsibility, too, thought Frankie. And you keep her away from her father, who would certainly welcome the chance of exercising his responsibility for his daughter.

'Well, I thought you should know about it, as you made Julie part of my job here. And I wouldn't want her to get hurt for lack of a little advice.'

'I appreciate that, Frankie. I'll have a little talk with her. But I still think that experience is the best teacher. Now let's talk about something less solemn. I managed to see the new play at the Haymarket on Saturday night. Mother insisted on my going, as she knows how much I love the theatre, and she had an old friend there to chat with. It was splendidly acted. A little shocking, perhaps, but then we're so behind the times here.'

She went on to discuss the play, and then the shops she had visited. Lying on the couch, in a pale green dress, her face alight with animation as she talked, her air of fragility as appealing as ever, she was as delightful to look at as the daffodils in the bowl behind her, and Frankie melted towards her, as always. She had brought back a filmy black nightdress for Julie which had evoked a rapturous response, and a polo-necked flame-coloured sweater for Frankie.

'I thought that would just suit your boyish style, Frankie,' she had said, her head on one side, an affectionate smile on her face.

What Caroline said to Julie about her Don Juan Frankie did not know, but about two weeks later she said casually, 'Oh, by the way, Frankie, I've met Julie's beau. Bumped into them coming out of The Old Pantry in Mynelly last Saturday, and insisted on taking them back in for another coffee. I quite liked him. A lot older than Julie, but that's all to the good. He's the owner of several good restaurants, one in Marlbury which I know, and he's doing rather well, I imagine. A man with some drive. Most reassuring.'

The Forsaken Garden

And so it was left. But when Don Birchington called to fetch Julie one evening in April and was drawn into the sitting-room by Caroline to have a drink while he waited, Frankie found him far from reassuring. He was a big coarse-grained man, with a red face, sleek black hair, and alert eyes above a ready smile. His dinner jacket looked as though it was due to be sent to the cleaners. He had a hearty manner and ran his eye over Frankie with quick expertise. She had met his type before, and guessed him to be at least twenty years older than Julie. How could Caroline view him so favourably and be so untroubled by the fact that her daughter was out almost every night until a late hour, and had brought home an appalling report from her school at Easter? But they were laughing and bantering like old friends, Caroline responding to his flattery like a dancer to the sound of music.

'Well, it's obvious where Julie gets her good looks from, Mrs. Falkland. A bit hard on her, with such stiff competition.'

'I can't compete with youth,' said Caroline gaily. 'But I enjoy my view from the side-lines. Hullo, darling. How pretty you look!' said Caroline as Julie came in.

And Julie did indeed look attractive, with her fair hair taken back smoothly to curve round in a soft coil over one bare shoulder. The style suited her small features, and her fair colouring showed up to advantage against the white material of her long, smooth-fitting dress. With diamanté drop earrings and diamanté necklace, the schoolgirl was quite eclipsed, only a few soft wisps of hair at the nape of her neck hinting at her youth.

'Worth waiting for,' said Don, his eyes lingering on her.

'Mummy, can I borrow your little fur cape? It would be just right.'

'There's blackmail for you!' said Caroline. 'Waiting until the last minute, knowing I couldn't spoil the picture by refusing. Frankie, be an angel and fetch it, will you? It's in my right-hand clothes cupboard, at the end.'

The cupboard was an enormous, walk-in affair on one side of the window, with a matching one on the other side. It was full of clothes, many carefully wrapped in Polythene covers, and all of them, Frankie did not doubt, expensive, for Caroline's clothes had a cut and style which set her apart.

It was Don who placed the mink cape over Julie's bare shoulders, and then stood back, admiring her with a possessive, almost gloating air.

They were just leaving when Rolf arrived. After a few brief exchanges, he went off to his father's room.

'Oh dear,' sighed Caroline. 'I can feel the temperature drop when Rolf comes in. Such a contrast after seeing those two happy young people going out to enjoy themselves. That little daughter of mine is really getting a very attractive young minx. I wish Rolf didn't come so often to chill the air.'

'Well, he doesn't trouble us much with his company,' said Frankie, looking out of the window at a white lilac tree in the garden whose blooms gleamed palely in the dusk.

'I fancy he's thawing out a little with you, though,' said Caroline, and Frankie was surprised at her quick appreciation of this fact, since she was away so much and never lingered when Rolf was about.

'Perhaps.'

'What do you make of him?'

'I really don't know him well enough to say.'

'He hates me,' said Caroline sadly. 'He does,' she added, silencing Frankie's protest. 'I must have failed him somewhere to make him so suspicious of me. But I still have hopes of Tracey. I saw them in Marlbury the other week, having lunch together. He seemed to be enjoying himself. The right woman might have a softening effect on Rolf. Anyway, I'm going to try a little strategy. I shall ask Tracey here more often, at the times Rolf usually comes to see his father. Propinquity's a great matchmaker. Although Rolf and I are not good friends, and nobody regrets that more than I, there's nothing I'd like better than to see him happily married. Living in that cottage all on his own. It's an unnatural way of life. No wonder he seems so grim. Don't you think my little strategy might pay dividends?'

'I wouldn't know. Rolf is a man who betrays so little of his feelings. But he knows his own mind, I'm sure, and I doubt whether other people's strategies would influence him.'

'We'll see. Julie tells me you're going to a concert in Marlbury with some of the clan next Saturday. Who's going?'

'Debbie, Barry, Aunt Gwen, Rolf and Tracey. It's a performance of Elgar's *Dream of Gerontius* and Barry's friend, Evan, is singing a solo part. He has a fine tenor voice, I'm told.'

'I don't go for choral music myself. But then I'm not Welsh. Aunt Gwen? You're getting well in with them, Frankie.'

'More with Debbie. She's shown me some good walks round here. I like her.'

'Yes, she's a nice young thing. But I shall be away next weekend. If you're going to be out, perhaps I ought not to go and leave Trevor alone.'

'Mrs. Filey's reliable. When Rolf told Mr. Falkland about the concert, he insisted on my taking a ticket. But of course I'll stay if you really want me to.'

'No, dear. I shan't hear of it. You go and enjoy yourself. You have little enough fun here, and if that's your idea of enjoyment, I'd be the last to put anything in the way. We'll see how Trevor is. He's seemed weaker lately, and I don't want to ask Mrs. Filey to give up her Saturday evenings too often. She likes to go to see her sister at the weekend. But don't you worry. I'll fix something.'

But Caroline had made Frankie feel guilty, although she knew that Trevor Falkland would never allow her to stay home on his account and miss the concert. And it wouldn't hurt Julie to stay in for once if Mrs. Filey wished to see her sister.

Caroline gathered up some magazines, took her little transistor wireless set and said a little wistfully, 'I feel tired this evening. I think I'll spend the evening in my room. Don't let the family steal you from me, Frankie.'

'No danger. I wish the divisions weren't there, though.'

'So do I. The trouble is, I've the wrong blood in my veins, and I'm considered far too young to be a good wife to Trevor. But it's a tremendous help, having you with me. I can't tell you how much I appreciate your warm heart and your loyalty, dear.'

Alone, Frankie tried to settle down to a book, but felt her concentration wandering. Restless, vaguely troubled, she felt homesick for the first time since she had come to Riverdale. She would have given a lot for an evening with Nick's cool mind, or a session with Grandma Rainwood who was rock-firm herself and who somehow seemed to firm up the ground under your feet, too.

The clock was striking ten when Rolf came into the sitting-room. He looked troubled.

'The old man's not in his usual chess form tonight,' he said. 'We've left the game to finish next time.'

'Does he want anything?'

'I've just asked Mrs. Filey to take him a whisky and milk. He's so confoundedly independent. Wouldn't let me help him to bed.'

'I can understand that. Once you give in, you're lost.'

'You look a bit peaky. Anything wrong?'

'Nothing specific. Think I'll have a short walk before I go to bed. I feel a bit keyed up. Don't know why.'

'Wouldn't mind a stretch myself. Don't see myself as exactly a soothing influence on you, so I'll leave it to you to decide whether our steps shall go in the same direction.'

He looked at her with a teasing expression, and she flushed and said, 'Let's go along the river as far as the bridge.'

A full moon lit their way across the garden. In daylight the neglected garden of Riverdale could be depressing, but by moonlight it gained a certain wild magic. They walked along a narrow path through a shrubbery so overgrown that in places they had to push back the bushes to get through. They skirted a thicket of bamboos, and Rolf took her hand as she stumbled down the broken stone steps to the remains of a hard tennis court. The wire netting surround was rusted and broken down along two sides, and had vanished completely from the other two, although a few small pieces still lurked in the long grass nearby to trap the unwary. Grass and weeds had grown through the tarmac surface of the court, and the wooden seat at the side lurched drunkenly. Beyond it lay what had once been a rose garden, and a few straggling roses still emerged from the tangle of weeds to remind the visitor of past glories. In the centre stood a small stone cherub on a pedestal with half of his face missing and one arm broken off. This last was a recent loss, and Frankie stooped to pick up the fallen limb from the ground.

'Poor cherub,' she said. 'Soon, he'll have crumbled away completely. This must have been a lovely garden once, Rolf.'

'Yes. My father loved it. But it was getting ahead of him before he had his stroke, and the old gardener became a passenger. Since my father's illness, nothing has been done at all. Caroline sacked the gardener, and didn't want to be bothered with getting another. It wouldn't have been easy to find one, anyway.'

'A pity. There's something so sad about a neglected garden. You can't help feeling it's haunted by ghosts of happier times. People laughing and playing on the tennis court, taking out that old punt on the river, picking the roses. Did you ever know it like that, Rolf?'

'No. This hasn't been my home for years, though. I left here as soon as I started earning my own living, and before then I was away at boarding school and college. In the early days of school holidays there was some effort at entertaining here, but

The Forsaken Garden

Caroline never took to the people round here or to country life. Just not interested. She'll sell the place and go back to London as soon as my father dies.'

He spoke in a cold, detached voice. Frankie put the arm of the cherub on the base of the pedestal and they walked on down to the dilapidated boat-house which still housed the few rotting timbers of a small punt.

'Would you be sorry? To see the house go, I mean,' she said as they paused by the river.

'Sorry? Good heavens, no!' he said bitterly. 'This garden symbolises to me the life here. My father's life. A good design obliterated by weeds, choked by jungle growth, disintegrating like that stone figure. A history of defeat and failure in all that matters. I hate the place. It makes me want to rage, and weep.'

Against such intensity of feeling, she felt helpless. Nothing she could say seemed relevant. He had never lifted the mask of urbanity in her presence before, and the sudden lightning glimpse of savage bitterness beneath made a frightening stranger of him. At last, she said tentatively, 'Why do you say your father's life is a failure, Rolf? I know his life is ruined now by his health, but before then . . .'

'There's nothing more futile than tracking back. Forget it. By the way, who was that oily-looking wolf escorting young Julie?'

She told him, and added, 'I'm a bit worried about Julie. Caroline seems to think it's quite all right for her to be running around with him every night and most of the weekend. She's hardly ever in, and nobody knows where she is. Caroline's away a good deal, and never asserts any authority over the girl. I'm all for freedom, but Julie's only seventeen. I'd like your father to take a hand, but Caroline insists that he mustn't be worried. Is she right? Would I be wrong to discuss it with him? I sometimes think he'd welcome more of Julie's company, but she seems scared of him.'

'She's been conditioned to it by Caroline. It's made the old man unhappy, seeing Julie grow up into a stranger. Another failure. But Caroline wanted it that way, and what Caroline wants, she gets.'

'You're unfair to her, Rolf. She's very kind and always puts your father's health first. If I've any criticism, it is that she's too kind where Julie's concerned.'

'Or just doesn't want to be bothered? But we'll not duscuss Caroline. She employs you and I understand your attitude. You're very young. There are things here that you couldn't possibly understand. But you're intelligent, too, and I'm afraid you've embarked on a voyage of discovery that may prove very disillusioning. Or perhaps not. If you could retain the blinkers that inexperience puts on you, you might survive with your rosy picture intact.'

'This division between the family. It's so wrong and unnecessary. It makes Caroline unhappy, I know.'

'My dear child, don't talk about things you know nothing about. There is no division in the family, apart from the inescapable fact that the respective parties have very little in common, that's all.'

'You're not going to deny that there's a division between you and Caroline, are you?'

'No. But that is none of your business.'

'Quite. I can't help sympathising with her, though. She has a lot to put up with, and she never lets it get her down.'

'I agree that Caroline is very skilful at never letting other people get her down or, indeed, bother her at all.'

'You twist my words to fit your own uncharitable feelings about her.'

'Oh, for heaven's sake don't start crusading for Caroline. She doesn't need your support, I assure you,' he said impatiently.

His use of the word crusading reminded her of Nick's warning, but she was too annoyed now to be cautious. She plunged in.

'I don't like vindictive people who thrive on enmity. Caroline's not strong, she has all the worry of your father's health to bear, as well as her mother's, and she's always bright and kind and generous, yet you have to cast another shadow on her life by your cruelty.'

'What cruelty? Caroline and I are always most polite to each other, on the few occasions when we can't avoid meeting.'

'There you are. Why should you avoid meeting her? Why shouldn't you try to help her instead of denigrating her?'

They had been walking along the river path, and he stopped now and caught her shoulders in a grip that hurt.

'Now look here, young woman. Caroline is my stepmother. I've known her since I was thirteen years old. You have been here barely three months. So don't presume to lecture me about her. I didn't bring up the subject of Caroline. I never discuss her with anybody. You brought up her attitude to Julie and asked me whether you should discuss it with my father. I had to tell you that Julie's a stranger to him because Caroline wants it that way, and if you try to cross Caroline, you'll be in trouble.'

'Nonsense,' said Frankie, furious at being unable to throw off his grip. 'Caroline and I are the best of friends. And shall remain so. She needs friends, heaven knows! And if you don't let me go, I shall kick you.'

'Temper.' And then, totally unexpectedly, he laughed, and released her. 'I forgot how young you are. For a girl who's been out in the world earning her own living in a tough profession, you've kept the bloom of innocence surprisingly intact, though.'

'If you think I'm a simpleton, just say so,' she snapped.

'Not a simpleton. And I tend to forget how good an actress Caroline is, too. I'm surprised she didn't make more of a success of acting. I'm not surprised that you didn't, though. *Ingénues* are a little out of fashion these days.'

Frankie's temper was of the quick sort that went up like a rocket and often came down just as quickly, and with his last remark Rolf had really hit her on the raw. She turned on him like a spitting cat.

'No wonder Caroline has given up all hope of bridging the gap between you. I'm truly sorry for her. A stepchild like you would have defeated an angel. If you're so hard and cruel and autocratic now, you were doubtless ill-natured and unmanageable from the first. But I don't have to put up with your sarcastic tongue, and from now on the less I see of you, the better.'

'As you wish,' he said calmly.

Speechless with anger, Frankie turned back along the river path and found herself in the rose garden again before her rage subsided into a miserable anger with herself for losing control and with him for his mocking tongue. *Ingénues are a little out of fashion these days.* She could hear that producer now, his voice cold with contempt.

'If you find it so hard to get under the skin of a part, Miss Barbury, why on earth do you purport to be an actress? Bianca is a strumpet, not a love-sick *ingénue*. Try again.' They had gone over the scene six times, and once he had come on the stage and given a cruel imitation of her to the amusement of the rest of the cast. In the end, he had reduced her to pulp, and had gone on to the next act with a shrug of his shoulders that indicated that she was past praying for. She had assumed that it was too small a part to make it worth his while to seek another actress for it, and she had stuck out the month of their run.

The battered cherub, pale in the moonlight, sad symbol of the erosion of time, reminded her of the savage unhappiness of Rolf's remarks about the garden; hard and cruel he might be, but he, too, had been deeply hurt on his father's behalf and must be credited with some humanity, however hard to find. The long tendrils of a rose caught at her tweed coat and she scratched her hand in trying to disentangle herself. She took the path through what had once been a tree-lined walk, thinking it would be easier than the path through the shrubbery, but here, too, brambles had encroached, and her stockings suffered. She was startled by two glowing eyes as she emerged. A large black cat was sitting on a rusty roller which was half submerged in a tangle of grass and weed. As Frankie approached, the cat leapt down and streaked away into the undergrowth.

Oppressed by the old feeling of inadequacy, smarting from her battle with Rolf, she quickened her steps towards the house away from that derelict garden which held no magic that night, only a melancholy picture of past beauty decayed, past hopes and effort obliterated by time's relentless tide.

7
A Truce

To avoid being collected by Rolf on the following Saturday, Frankie cycled over to Mynelly and went to the concert with Deborah and her parents in the family car driven by Barry. Rolf arrived just after them with Tracey. Frankie greeted him with cool politeness and put as much space between them as she could during the evening. She enjoyed the performance, in which Evan distinguished himself, and afterwards found that the ever hospitable Mynelly branch of the Falkland family had laid on a cold late supper for them all. They rounded off the evening with a sing-song, Deborah played the piano and Evan leading the singing of the old welsh songs. It was nearly one o'clock when the party finally broke up.

'You can't cycle back at this time of the night, Frankie,' said Rolf briefly. 'Better leave your bike here and collect it another day. I'll drop you home.'

It was the only remark he had addressed to her that evening after the first polite greeting, a feat not difficult in the company of such voluble people.

'Of course I can cycle. I shall enjoy it.'

'In the rain?' he asked drily.

'It's pouring, dear,' said Aunt Gwen. 'Best do as Rolf says. I wouldn't like to think of you cycling along those dark lanes at this hour and in such weather. It's not much out of Rolf's way, either.'

And there was little she could do but accept Rolf's offer. She sat in the back of the car, leaving Tracey beside Rolf until he dropped the latter off at her uncle's hotel.

'Are you going to stay in the back?' he asked after Tracey had dived for the shelter of the hotel.

'I'm very comfortable.'

'Right,' he said shortly, and drove on.

The rain was sheeting down and the wiper could hardly keep the windscreen clear. The cottage where Rolf lived was about half way between Mynelly and Riverdale. Deborah had pointed it out to her one day when they were walking. She glanced down the lane as they passed. She could just see the porch light gleaming through the trees. An odd, solitary sort of life. A woman came in from the village to do the cleaning, Deborah had said. The silence in the car was oppressive. Looking at the back of his head, she wished that she could be more detached about him, and wondered whether she would ever learn to put a discreet bridle on her tongue instead of always having things out. She had gained nothing by losing her temper the other night, and rushing in with accusations which, while she believed them to be true, would have been better left unsaid since they were bound to make future contacts difficult, and in the circumstances in which she found herself, such contacts were unavoidable.

The night was inky black, the rain a silvered sheet in their headlights. The swish of the wheels, the monotonous click of the wiper, the whoosh of spray as their near-side wheels caught the river of water at the side of the road, did nothing to lighten the oppressiveness of the atmosphere inside the car. Then, with the suddenness of a meteor, a car flashed out of a side road straight into their path. Frankie thought they must hit it, but Rolf swung the car off the road on to a providentially flat area of rough grass, they slewed round in an arc and the car came to rest facing away from the road, rocking like a boat. Rolf swore.

'Blazing idiot!'

'He must have been drunk,' said Frankie.

'Lucky for us the ground was open here.'

'What happened to the other car? I couldn't see.'

'I was a bit preoccupied myself, but he zig-zagged across the road and then went on, it seems. I'd like a few words with him. Didn't have a chance to get his number.' He lit a cigarette, turning as he did so. 'You all right?'

'Yes, thanks. It all happened too fast to be scared, anyway. You did well to control the car and get us out of that.'

'Don't know what we've got into, though,' said Rolf grimly as he lowered the window and looked out through the curtain of rain at the terrain. 'Looks like a near bog, and the longer we stay here the worse it'll be. Let's see what happens.'

He put the car into reverse, but the wheels spun in the mud and the car refused to move. After several abortive efforts to move it either backwards or forwards, he said, 'I'll have to make a survey. Hand over that raincoat, will you?'

A Truce

She passed him the raincoat from the seat beside her. The rain drumming on the roof sounded vindictive. When he returned from his investigations, he said, 'A few yards ahead it's a bit firmer. I'll try putting some brushwood down, and a couple of old sacks I've got in the boot. If that doesn't work I'll have to walk to the nearest telephone and see if I can get a breakdown van.'

'I'll give you a hand.'

'No, stay there. You'll get soaked, and it's several inches deep in mud.'

But Frankie was out, her coat collar turned up, making for the coppice visible in the headlights of the car a few yards off. The willow branches she broke off bore their buds along the length of the wood but the silvery soft texture which she had so loved to stroke as a child now resembled the coat of a drowned kitten. Rolf, nearby, was tearing off the lower branches of an alder.

'Don't you ever do as you're told?' he asked.

'Sometimes, when I'm asked. Seldom, when I'm told.'

'Two of us soaked now instead of one.'

'Don't crab,' said Frankie cheerfully. 'If it weren't for me, you'd be home and dry in your cottage by now.'

Somehow, the tensions within her had been released by the predicament they were in and the physical efforts needed to get them out of it. Introspection did not suit her; she was always happier when her nervous energy had physical outlets. So wet now that it no longer mattered, ankle deep in mud, she bent to her task with a will.

'That bracken might help,' said Rolf.

They rammed bracken and wood in front of the rear wheels of the car, and Rolf used the sacks for the front wheels. 'I'll push,' said Frankie as Rolf got in.

The car jerked, moved an inch, and then the wheels spun again.

'It nearly made it," said Frankie. 'A bit more under this right wheel and I think we'll do it.'

She slithered back to the coppice for some more bracken, and Rolf spotted an old rotten plank half hidden in the long grass which was a valuable addition. Pushing with all her strength as he put the car in gear again, she nearly fell over when it jerked forward, made the firmer ground ahead and was brought back onto the road. Running after it, she climbed into the seat beside Rolf, beaming triumphantly.

'We made it,' she said breathlessly.

He had switched on the interior light and was looking at her with a quizzical expression. The water was running off her short black hair in rivulets, and her legs and feet were plastered with mud. She peeled off her sodden, filthy gloves and accepted the dry, clean handkerchief he had unearthed from his jacket pocket to wipe her face. Rolf, in similar shape, mopped up as best he could with a leather from the car glove compartment.

'You're a good partner in a jam,' he said. 'I have known females who would have had a different approach. In fact, you even seem to have derived a certain enjoyment from it.'

'I like a challenge,' she said blithely.

He laughed and rubbed her tousled wet hair with a friendly hand.

'I'm learning. You can't stay on a high horse for long, anyway. I take it that the back seat no longer attracts you?'

'I prefer it here. I'm sorry if I blew my top the other evening. I know I said more than I should. You just happened to hit on a phrase my last producer used when blasting me with his scorn for my acting abilities, and it stung.'

'What phrase was that?'

She told him, and he raised his eyebrows.

'You as Bianca in *Othello*? A shocking bit of miscasting, surely. If the producer was responsible for that, he's the one who should have been blasted. You're just about the last person in the world to play a courtesan.'

'A good actress should be able to get inside the skin of any part.'

'A young girl with your looks, background and inexperience for a part like that? You can't turn a girl who looks like Peter Pan into a strumpet.'

'Make-up can do a lot, you know.'

'But can't change what's inside. Anyway, I'm sorry I trod on that particular corn, but there's more to it than that, Frankie, isn't there?'

'Yes. I can't take back what I said, because it was true, but I'm sorry I said it.'

'Why? I prefer honesty.'

'I said it was true, but perhaps it was only half true. I know so little of you, really. If you seem hard and cruel sometimes, I know I only see one facet of you and know nothing of the reasons behind your attitude to Caroline. What can we ever really know about other people? In depth, I mean. And half-knowledge can lead to half-truths. That's why I shouldn't have said all that I did, I'm sorry.'

'All right. Forget it. We'll agree to keep Caroline out of our conversation, since that seems to be the bone of contention. And heaven knows I don't want to discuss her. But I can't butter things up, Frankie. I can keep silent, but not pretend. And it is cool nerve, after three months' acquaintance with my family to lecture me on the nature of our relationships, don't you agree?'

'Yes. I meant well, though.'

'And the road to hell is paved with good intentions. Anyway, we'll sigh a truce and avoid the boggy places. Some day, though, Frankie, you'll have to choose where your alliance lies. There can be no compromise in this. You're shivering. High time to get you home to a hot bath. It's been quite an evening, one way and another.'

And, soaking in a hot bath some twenty minutes later, Frankie thought uneasily of his words, no compromise. She wished she understood him better. Wished she was not a victim of such conflicting emotions where he was concerned. And why couldn't he compromise? Members of any family had to compromise for the sake of reasonable harmony. It was that ruthlessness in him that she feared.

8
Remembrance of Things Past

As spring slipped into summer, Frankie found herself increasingly busy, for Caroline's mother needed more and more of Caroline's attention, and Trevor Falkland, although not complaining, seemed to Frankie to be losing ground fast. Now that better weather had come, he was able to spend more time in the garden, although the neglected state of the paths made their excursions difficult and limited in scope. Knowing that the state of the garden saddened him, she set about making one corner, at least, less of an eyesore, and this absorbed most of what little spare time she had. The rest, she spent mainly with Deborah, whose friendship she enjoyed. But behind all her activities, the main preoccupation of her mind was Rolf. Since the incident with the car, a slightly guarded friendship had been established between them, but she felt that at base it was Caroline who stood between them. On that subject their divergence was complete, and although not mentioned, it was there, like a trip-wire between them.

A little light was thrown on this enigmatic disturber of her peace of mind by Deborah one Saturday afternoon in June when they were walking in the foothills.

'He's never been quite one of us, though we all have a tremendous respect for Rolf. There's some inner reserve there which we all sense but can't define. But then we Welsh are very clannish and Rolf's not pure Welsh, as my father would put it.'

'I find him . . . difficult. So likeable sometimes, and so chilling at others. He puzzles me,' said Frankie.

'I think that, fundamentally, he's an unhappy and frustrated person,' said Deborah slowly. 'I've no tangible reason for saying that. I just feel it. And although he seems hard sometimes, I always remember how kind he was to me when I was a kid. Few boys would have much time for a cousin ten years their junior, but I can remember Rolf playing with me when I was only a toddler. I adored him. If he seems cold and unapproachable now, it's because he hides his feelings. And perhaps feels too much.'

'Caroline thinks Tracey might make a lot of difference to him.'

'I wouldn't know. He's very attractive, isn't he?'

'Yes. Has there ever been anybody? To account for his unhappiness, I mean.'

'Not that I know of. I remember one or two glamorous creatures in the past, but since his father's illness he seems to have played a lone hand. But I don't really know. He's a defensive person where his personal life's concerned. I hope it's not Tracey, though. That would mean he'd go to Canada and we'd lose him altogether.'

'I doubt whether he'd leave his father at this stage.'

'No. But I think he'll leave here after his father goes, anyway, and it may be that Tracey is the answer. Her father has offered Rolf a job in his company, you know. On the architectural side. It's a huge concern.'

'But the Falkland business surely means something to him. What makes you think he'll leave here anyway?'

'My father's sure he will. He says he'll do his best to keep him, because he's a clever architect and a good administrator as well, but he told me once that Rolf only came into the business because he felt he had to and because he was badly needed when Uncle Trevor was lost to them so suddenly, although originally he'd intended to go into practice as an architect. That's what he trained for. But Uncle Trevor's illness made a difference.'

'So it could be Tracey,' said Frankie slowly.

'What do you think of her? She's over at Riverdale quite a bit these days, I hear.'

'Yes. I like what little I know of her. Seems a straightforward person. Plenty of sex-appeal there. And she sometimes looks at Rolf as though she'd like to eat him,' added Frankie lightly, covering up the uncomfortable jabs which this conversation was administering.

'And Rolf?'

'Just friendly, with that kind of cool, bantering way he has.'

'Don't I know! A splendid method for standing you off.'

Frankie surprised an unhappy expression on Deborah's face, and was at a loss to know what to say. Treading delicately, she said, 'Well, it's a perverse world. I've only had my fingers burned once so far, and then not badly, so I don't consider myself an expert on such matters. As a matter of fact, I was inclined to be a bit sceptical about men and the love-trap until my sister Jenny married at a very unhappy time of her life and has been completely transformed. Now I'm inclined to think I could be wrong. That to love and be loved must be the greatest blessing of all.'

'Of course,' said Deborah simply. 'But all other males have somehow seemed dim to me beside my dynamic cousin, so my fingers will probably never be burned. Look. The first harebells I've seen. The summer's getting on.'

Deborah stooped to the little cluster of harebells beside the path, and Frankie took the hint and gave her attention to the countryside around them. They parted at the bus stop on the outskirts of Mynelly.

'Sure you won't come back to tea?' asked Deborah.

'I'd like to, Debbie, but Mrs. Filey's going to see her sister this evening and I must be in. Julie's going to a dance and Caroline's away.'

'As usual.'

'Her mother's got a cataract and is nearly blind. It's a great worry to Caroline.'

'Why doesn't she have her down here?'

'Well, you know how old people cling to their homes.'

'I shall be in trouble from Barry again for not bringing you back. He says you're allowing yourself to be put upon. And you've refused three invitations from him. What's wrong with his face, he says.'

'It's a very nice face, but I was tied up on the two evenings he asked me to go to a dance, and I couldn't go and watch him play cricket last Saturday because I'd just got a delivery of plants for the garden that had to be bedded in.'

'And who'd want to watch that boring game, cricket?' added Deborah, smiling.

'Tell him it's nothing personal and I'm sure he's found satisfactory substitutes. I'm very tied. It's not that I work long hours, but that I don't have any set hours.'

'Not to worry. Julie ought to take a hand with her father, though. And I'd always stand in any time. You know that.'

'Yes. Thanks, Debbie. But it is my job, after all. And I've grown fond of Mr. Falkland. I like being with him.'

Waving to Deborah from the platform of the bus, Frankie was conscious of a warm affection for this quiet unobtrusive girl who asked so little and was always ready to give. A striking contrast to Julie, thought Frankie darkly, for they had crossed swords that morning over the girl's attitude to her father.

'I can't go and sit with him. He gives me the shudders. He's so ugly. And I hate sick-rooms, anyway. I never know what to say to him, and it's all so depressing,' she had said.

And the argument that had followed had gone from bad to worse, although Julie was a cold little thing and never got rattled, only spiteful.

'I thought that was what you were paid for,' she had concluded with a little smile that had made Frankie want to reach for a stick.

While she was reading to Trevor Falkland that evening, Rolf came in. It was early for him.

'I'm driving up to London tonight, so thought I'd look in for an hour on my way. I had a letter from Miguel this morning, Dad. He's arriving at Heathrow at eight-thirty tomorrow morning. Thought I'd meet him and spend a few days in London with him before showing him a bit of the country.'

'How long is he staying?'

'Only a week. He can't spare longer. They're busy on the estate. A new irrigation plant's being installed."

'Will he have time to come here?'

'He's had his instructions from Grandma,' said Rolf, grinning. 'I'm bringing him down on Friday. He'll stay with me, and go back on Monday. His flight back is latish Monday evening.'

'Good. I'll be glad to see the boy. Don't go, Frankie. I'd like Rolf to hear you read this bit of Mark Twain. This girl brings books to life quite wonderfully, Rolf.'

'Splendid,' said Rolf, settling himself comfortably in an armchair.

A little confused by the gleam in his eyes, Frankie returned to the book and was soon oblivious of her audience, apart from the gratification of hearing Rolf's father chuckle delightedly now and again. When she had finished the chapter, Rolf said, 'Now I know why your chess is suffering, Dad. The stage's loss is your gain. I'd like to join the audience sometimes, if I'm permitted.'

'We'll see. Frankie's equally gifted at tragedy, comedy, poetry and prose. I enjoy it so much that I'm afraid I ask too much of her time.'

'And I enjoy acting without the bane of producers, and having all the good parts into the bargain,' said Frankie.

'I think you may have been wrong to quit the stage. That low, husky little voice of yours is a rare asset. But who am I to put such an idea into your head? Trying to saw off the bough on which I sit so happily,' said Trevor Falkland.

'The critics seemed to overlook my assets on the few occasions when I performed.'

'Critics!' Trevor Falkland dismissed them with scorn. 'Round it off with this, my dear,' he added, handing her a shabby book open at the requiem from *Cymbeline*. She had read it to him before. It was a piece of which he was particularly fond.

She moved her chair nearer to the window for a better light and began,

> Fear no more the heat o' the sun
> Nor the furious winter's rages;
> Thou thy worldly task hast done,
> Home art gone and ta'en thy wages:
> Golden lads and girls all must,
> As chimney-sweepers, come to dust.

She read on through its beautiful, melancholy conclusion, half in love with it herself, half protesting on this warm summer evening against its sad philosophy. But Trevor Falkland said, his eyes on Rolf, 'I find that comforting.'

Rolf nodded, but said nothing.

'Can I get you some coffee or something to eat, Rolf, before you go?' asked Frankie. 'You've a long drive in front of you.'

'No, thanks. I shall have dinner on the way. I'd better be off now.' He laid a hand on his father's shoulder for a moment. 'I'll leave you two to feast on words,' he added, then saluted Frankie with a smile and left them.

'Well, feast on words or not, we shall need more substantial victuals, too. Would you care for scrambled eggs for supper? And coffee? I thought we might have it on the trolley in here,' said Frankie.

'An excellent idea. Thank you, my dear.'

While she was in the kitchen there was a knock on the door. It was Tracey, who came in with her usual friendly air.

'I'm just getting some supper in the kitchen. Mr. Falkland and I are on our own tonight. Will you join us?' asked Frankie.

'On your own? Isn't Rolf here, then?'

'He's been. Left five minutes ago. He's on his way to London to meet a friend at the airport.'

'Well, he might have let me know!' exclaimed Tracey angrily.

'His movements are always a bit uncertain. He has a key and comes and goes at all times. Whenever he has an hour to spare, he spends it with his father.'

'But he was going to . . . I thought Caroline said . . .' She bit her lip and then said quickly, 'Oh, never mind. I guess there's been some misunderstanding. You're busy. I'll be on my way.'

'Do stay, Tracey, if you'd like to. We're only having a light meal of scrambled eggs and coffee. Mr. Falkland would be glad to see you.'

'No, I won't stop now, thanks all the same.'

'What about transport?' asked Frankie, knowing that Tracey usually came on the bus and was taken back by Rolf. 'There's no bus due for nearly an hour.'

'Oh, this benighted place! I really shall have to buy a car. I didn't think it would be worth while for the short time I'm over here, as I can borrow my uncle's car when he doesn't want it, and one or other of the Falklands is usually ready to oblige, but if Rolf's going to be unreliable . . .'

Her voice trailed away. She was evidently finding it difficult to hide her anger. It seemed hardly reasonable to look on Rolf as a chauffeur, though.

'There's the car-hire man in the village,' suggested Frankie.

Tracey went out to the hall to telephone. Frankie could not suppress a little impish amusement at this situation. It was Barry's opinion that Tracey purposely kept to a car-less state so that males willy-nilly had to act as escorts, and Frankie thought there might be some truth in this. For, as Barry said, she had driven a car ever since she was old enough to have a licence, and had enough money to buy a fleet of cars if she wished. 'A woman on the hunt,' Barry had said darkly. 'Dangerous. But the prey this time is an unusually elusive one, I fancy.'

'He'll be here in ten minutes,' said Tracey when she returned, 'so I'll just slip in and say good evening to Rolf's father before I go.'

When, after Tracey had gone, Frankie wheeled the supper trolley into Trevor Falkland's study, he said, 'Open the window a bit wider, my dear, will you? That sultry young women used a very cloying scent.'

Frankie leaned out of the window to watch the rooks wheeling about the old elm tree.

'It's a fine evening for Rolf's drive,' she said.

'Yes. He'll enjoy a few days with Miguel. They're great friends. Miguel's his cousin, on his mother's side, and they've known each other since they were children. My son's always been very attached to his Spanish relatives, and to Spain. He spends all his holidays there. A long allegiance, dating, I think, from the year he spent with his grandmother in Mallorca after his mother died.'

'He's never said anything about it to me. In fact, I had the impression that he was essentially a loner. But Rolf never talks much about himself, anyway.'

'You and he get on well, though?'

'Yes. Very well. But I find him . . . complex. Difficult to get to know. He keeps his defences intact.'

'Yes. You would find him different in Mallorca, perhaps. Here, he's never relaxed. And he's learned to give nothing away. He had a far from ideal childhood. And hard lessons then stay with you and mould you.' He sighed as he picked up his knife and fork, his right hand fumbling, nearly useless, but she knew better than to offer assistance. She had cut the toast into small squares to make his task easier.

'Well, however detached he is with everybody else, he's obviously devoted to you,' she said, thinking to cheer him a little.

'And that's something I can be profoundly grateful for, knowing I've done nothing to deserve it. Rolf has little to thank me for; fond as I am of him, I've really spoilt his life.'

'Oh no!' exclaimed Frankie, shocked at his bitterness.

'Well, it's too late to do anything about that now. It would have been better for him if I'd left him in Mallorca with his grandmother after his mother died. But I was selfish. I wanted him here with me.'

'Naturally.'

'He was nine when his mother died. We lived in America. I'd met her in Mallorca when I was on holiday there. A beautiful island. A beautiful girl. Love at first sight. It's nice to have one idyll in your life to look back to. I only have to smell the sage and the lavender in the garden to be back on the woodland paths round the Mallorcan cliffs, with that blue, blue sea and the Mediterranean pines. Know it at all?'

'No. I've had no opportunity to travel so far.'

'The lower slopes of the mountains and the foothills are covered with maquis; low-growing shrubs and herbal plants which have a delicious, pungent scent in the hot sun. You must go there one day, my dear.'

'Yes, I'd love to.'

'Splendid place for plant-hunting, Mallorca. And the mainland of Spain offers even more scope. Particularly Andalusia. Ask Rolf about it some time. He knows it like the back of his hand.'

He had pushed his plate aside, the meal half eaten, and Frankie poured him some coffee. It was unusual for him to talk at this length about personal matters.

'When Rolf's mother was alive, we always went back to Mallorca for our holidays,' he went on. 'It was a quiet place then. Still is in what they call their winter, Rolf says. But I wouldn't know. All this was before the tourist explosion, of course. I came back to Wales when my wife died. I'd left when I was twenty and I'd been away eighteen years. The war had taken place in the interval. There were some big changes, but down here, not so apparent. Funny, this homing instinct.'

'And Rolf came with you.'

'He stayed with his grandmother in Mallorca for the best part of a year while I found my bearings here again. Then I wanted him back, and his grandmother very generously offered to come here and make a home for us while the boy was so young. She was widowed then. Nine is no age, after all, and Rolf was very unhappy at leaving Mallorca and his relatives there. She made a home for us here during the next few years. I bought this house because I've always liked plants and gardening, and it seemed a good place for a boy. Grandma Albyon went back to Mallorca when I married Caroline. So you see that Rolf had a rather unsettled existence during the most impressionable years of his life. He had a hard time, one way and another. I wanted to do so much for him, and I've spoilt his life. Ironical, really.'

'I simply don't believe that. And nor does Rolf, I'm sure.'

'I've talked too much. You have a sympathetic way with you, my dear. I forget you're young and are concerned with the present, not an elderly man's past.'

'But the past affects the present, doesn't it? And I'm glad you've told me what you have about Rolf. I find him so hard to understand, and it helps to know something of his past. In some ways, I like him so much. In others, he . . . almost scares me. And I'm not easily scared. He can seem so hard and ruthless and suspicious of people's motives. So contradictory, and, somehow, always at war.'

'The passionate pride of his grandmother's people. And an abrasive childhood to sharpen the steel. What can you expect? Nothing comfortable, for sure. But Isabella Albyon holds the key to Rolf's heart and mind, if anyone does. Now, instead of dissecting my difficult son, shall we spend half an hour with Jane Austen? Far more restful.'

And they turned to *Emma*.

9
A Party

WHEN Caroline learned that Miguel was coming to see her husband the next weekend, she decided that they would have a small supper party on the Saturday. It was the first entertaining which she had done since Frankie's arrival, a fact which Frankie found rather surprising in view of Caroline's gay and charming personality, but which she put down to fatigue on Caroline's part through the pressures on her just then. This supposition was confirmed by Caroline when she discussed the party with Frankie.

'I don't really feel that I have the energy to cope with a party, but Trevor wishes to show Miguel some hospitality and would like to have his family over to meet him again. It's five years since he was last here. I think it's all too much for Trevor, of course, but if he wants it, I must do my best. I feel pretty knocked up myself just now, though, and I do find my worthy in-laws so *exhausting*.'

'Mrs. Filey and I can see to everything behind the scenes. How many will be coming?'

'Let me see. The Mynelly household numbers four, then there's Lloyd, Rolf, Tracey, Miguel. I don't know whether Julie would like Don to come. But perhaps not. I don't think he'd fit in with the Falklands. That means we'll be a dozen in all. Do you think you and Mrs. Filey can manage that?'

'Of course. Don't you worry. Just relax and leave it to us.'

'How good you are, Frankie! What should I do without you now? I don't want to shift my mother to a convalescent home, but if things go on like this, I may have to.'

And Caroline did look like a wilted flower herself as she removed a vase of drooping delphiniums.

That week, after a long spell of unsettled, chilly weather, it turned hot, and on the Saturday of the party the temperature soared to the eighties. The heat seemed to bear hardly on Trevor Falkland, and when Frankie took him a cup of tea that afternoon, she thought he looked exhausted before the party had even started. He was painfully and slowly writing a letter, using his left hand.

'Can't I do that for you?' she asked.

'Thank you, my dear, but I can manage. Wish I'd learned to be ambidexterous when I was young, though. This letter to Grandma Albyon is long overdue. I want to give it to Miguel to take back with him.'

'I thought you were going to rest this afternoon.'

'I had a short rest. And, after all, I spend most of my life resting now. It's years since we did any entertaining. I'm quite looking forward to it.'

And when the time came, he seemed to draw strength from the occasion and played the host with a warmth which gave her a glimpse of an earlier Trevor Falkland.

There was one thing to be said for entertaining the Falkland family, thought Frankie; there were no awkward blanks. From the word go, they were at it. Lively, as voluble as ever, the usually quiet sitting-room was soon noisy with laughter and passionate discussion, calling for no effort from host or hostess to prevent things from falling flat. And Miguel took to it all like a duck to water. When Rolf introduced him to her, Frankie could see the likeness between the cousins. The same dense black hair and dark eyes. But Miguel was shorter and of sturdier build than Rolf, with flashing white teeth and a courteous charm which was disarming. He was a little younger than Rolf, she guessed, and far more anxious to please, with none of Rolf's cool detachment. Frankie, busy behind the scenes until they all went in to supper, found herself sitting next to him then, and enjoyed his company.

'Caroline tells me that you have been on the stage, Frankie,' he said in his precise English. 'And that now you have come like an angel to her aid.'

'Caroline makes too much of me on both counts.'

'She is lovely. So young and gay. Julie has grown into a pretty young woman, too. She was a child when I last saw her.'

'Have you enjoyed your week here?'

'But so much! Rolf is a splendid guide. He and I have enjoyed many good times together. And the weather has been not bad.'

'Not bad? We call this marvellous. Actually hot.'

'Hot? No. Just pleasant. I have been so struck,' he went on, helping himself to another cutlet of salmon at Caroline's invitation, 'with the singing of Rolf's relatives. That song just now. "Come back to the hills and valleys." It was so good. The harmony.'

'Yes. The Welsh seem to sing as naturally as they talk, and both of Mr. Falkland's brothers belong to a choral society.'

'I like these people. They are, how do you say, lively. Not closed up. Rolf and I were in the village inn last night. They were talking about Welsh nationalism. It got so heated. Then they all finished up singing the Welsh national anthem. It was so enjoyable,' he concluded with a flashing smile.

Julie put on the record player in the hall after supper, and they all danced, with the exception of Gwendolyn and Elwyn, who kept Trevor Falkland company in the sitting-room. Caroline seemed to have found renewed energy that evening, and danced with greater zest than her daughter, who appeared a little bored with the proceedings. Miguel partnered them all in turn, then seemed to favour Frankie, so that Barry said when he took her off for a quick-step, 'Can't get a look in this evening. That Spanish charm's dangerous. Better watch it.'

'Come on, slow-coach. You're behind the beat,' said Frankie, and he grinned and took up the challenge.

But towards the end of the evening, even Frankie's energy began to wane. She had started very early that day, helping Mrs. Filey with the cooking, and the heat had depleted her vitality. Conscious of a slight headache and a need for cooler air, she slipped out on to the terrace. The night was still and warm. There was no moon, and the stars glittered in a velvety black sky. Moving cautiously along the uneven flagstones and down the crumbling steps, she crossed the lawn to the small clearing she had made by the river. Here she had cleaned up and mended a wooden seat, planted a semi-circle of pinks and cut back the overgrown shrubs. And it was here that she brought Trevor Falkland when weather permitted. She leaned on the back of the seat, her eyes now accustomed to the dark, and watched the silky surface of the river.

She had been there for only a few minutes when voices nearby startled her. They came from the other side of the thicket of shrubs and trees.

'Rolf, didn't you hear me call?' It was Tracey's voice.

'No.'

'I nearly ricked my ankle on that rough paving.'

'It's a dark night for wandering about in this wilderness.'

'I'd say! But I wanted a word with you. Why are you avoiding me?'

'I wasn't aware of doing so.'

'And why didn't you let me know you wouldn't be here last Saturday night?'

'Why should I?'

'Out of common politeness. Caroline said you'd be here and would like to see those photographs my father sent me of the ranch he's just bought near Vancouver.'

'I'm sorry, Tracey. I seem to remember Caroline mentioning them in a vague sort of way, but I made no commitment.'

'No. You never make any commitment, do you?' said Tracey bitterly.

Frankie heard the sound of a match being struck. She could not escape. The river barred her way in front, dense shrubs surrounded her, and the only path back was the one on which Tracey and Rolf were standing.

'Tell me, Tracey, why do you come to Riverdale so often in the evenings now?' asked Rolf after a pause.

'Because Caroline told me you'd welcome my company after your sessions with your father, which were apt to be depressing, she said.'

'But do you really think that I can't make my own arrangements for light relief, if needed?'

'You mean you didn't suggest it, or hint at it?'

'No.'

'Well, I like that! What does Caroline think she's doing?'

'Playing matchmaker, perhaps,' said Rolf ironically.

'This is the twentieth century, not the nineteenth.'

'Quite.'

'Rolf, I must speak plainly. I find this too humiliating. You know how I feel about you. You must know. You're no fool.'

'I'm sorry, Tracey. It's no go.'

'But we could have such a good life together. Dad took a liking to you when he was over at Christmas. You'd have a job worthy of your capabilities, instead of this tin-pot construction business of the Falklands. The open air life is grand and would suit you. There's room to breathe in Canada. And you find me attractive enough. I've seen your eyes on me and I'm not a child. And for the first time in my life, I'm really in love. Why else do you think I've kept putting off going home? Dad expects it. Caroline wants it. Why not?'

'We're good friends, Tracey. Leave it at that.'

'No. Where I come from, we don't mince words. I want to get this straight. Just where do you stand? Caroline made me think . . .'

A Party

'Caroline knows nothing about my personal affairs.'

'Why did she encourage me to think you felt as I do, then? Always coupling our names, acting as though it was a foregone conclusion.'

'Wishful thinking, perhaps.'

'Why? Why me? She doesn't know me that well.'

'You have the inestimable advantage, my dear Tracey, of living on the other side of the Atlantic and you've made it clear that that is where you would take me. Caroline would be so happy to have the Atlantic between her and me.' His voice was as dry as sawdust.

'Oh. I see. That's how it is. Well, I don't take kindly to being used as a pawn in Caroline's game. It's humiliating.'

'I know. I'm really sorry. I mean that.'

'O.K. But Rolf, there's something between us. Couldn't it be more? Doesn't the life I'm offering tempt you at all? My father's a millionaire. I'm not saying you're mercenary, but it would be a fine opportunity for you. We could be happy there, I know.'

'My dear, I can't say that marriage appeals to me very much. I've seen a few wrecks. I like my freedom. But if I do marry, it will be because I love someone so much that I can't do anything else. As for my working life—I can make my own way, and prefer to do so. I have my own plans, but while my father's alive my hands are tied. Marriage doesn't come into them.'

'All right, then. You're too stubbornly independent, but I don't blame you for that. I'm a bit that way myself. But if you can't feel that grand passion for me, there are less exalted pleasures to be enjoyed.'

'I don't like messy situations. And it would only make things more hurtful for you in the end.'

'I'll risk that.'

'No, Tracey. I like you too much to play with you. You see, you wouldn't be playing. Go back home and forget it.'

'As if it were that easy! Why are you so darned scrupulous, Rolf? Perhaps it's because you're made of stone. Then, I suppose, it's easy.'

'Well, let's say that's the way I am, shall we?'

'Not true. There's fire underneath that cool surface. Some wretched girl will be warmed by it, I suppose. Perhaps your scruples come from your Spanish ancestry. Caroline was telling me that your grandmother is Spanish.'

'Mallorcan.'

'Same blood. And in Spain they still have chaperones, and a couple have to be almost at the altar before they're left on their own. Are you like that, Rolf? Drawing a line between ladies, and the others. And treating them accordingly.'

'It's a system not without its merits.'

'Well, why put me in with the ladies?'

'Because, my dear Tracey, that's where you belong. And we've spent long enough on this subject. Come in and have a drink.'

'That's really and truly final, Rolf?'

'Really and truly, dear,' he said gently.

'All right. I've never doubted that you know your own mind. I shall go back home next week. Will you write?'

'No. I said, forget it. You'll be able to do that more quickly without reminders from me.'

They were moving away and Frankie could not hear Tracey's reply. She lingered a few minutes longer, then went back to the house. There she found Tracey dancing with Miguel, and Rolf with Deborah. Barry made a bee-line for Frankie, and she tried to whip up an energy to match his.

Lloyd, the middle one of the three Falkland brothers, considered himself a good dancer, but his dancing dated from earlier days. When he asked Julie to put on a good old-fashioned waltz, she had difficulty in finding one, but finally unearthed an old record of the Merry Widow waltz, and Lloyd swept Caroline a bow and they circled the hall alone before the others joined in. Rolf claimed Frankie. It was the first time she had danced with him that evening. They both slipped into the lilt of the music easily.

'Tired?' he asked, when they had circled the hall in silence.

'A little. But enjoying this too much to want to talk.'

He smiled and drew her a little more firmly into his arm.

'You shouldn't let Caroline run you off your feet,' he said when the record stopped and Lloyd went across to play it again.

'I don't. I like Miguel. I think the party's been a success, don't you?'

'Yes. Can't remember when we last had a party here. The old man's stood up to it well, but it's nearly midnight and I think he's had enough.'

'Yes. And the heat tires him.'

'Mmm. Hope it's a bit cooler tomorrow. Miguel and I are going up Cader.'

'What energy!'

'It's a grand view from the top.'

'Is Miguel a good climber?'

'Yes. We've done a bit in the Sierra Nevada together. Cader's not much more than a mild hill walk up the path we're taking, though. Perhaps you'd like to do it with me one day, and see the best view in Wales from the summit.'

'I'd love to.'

'It'll probably be strenuous enough to keep us from fighting, anyway,' he said with a smile as they started to dance again.

In his arms she had no wish to talk. It was good to put her questioning mind to rest and give herself up to the happy lilt of the music and a physical harmony with him that made their differences irrelevant.

10
A Touch of Glory

It was not until one Saturday at the end of July that Rolf took Frankie on the climb up Cader Idris. It was one of Caroline's rare weekends at Riverdale, and she had seemed a little reproachful when she heard of the Cader project, although rounding off her lack of enthusiasm with a firm declaration that it would do Frankie good to have a day out and she would certainly hold the fort during her absence.

Their way took them first through foothills where the grass was emerald green and ferns lined the banks of a rushing stream. It was a day of cloud and fitful sunshine, with the air cool and fresh. The only sounds to break the silence were the running water and the occasional baa of a sheep from the flock grazing on the lower slopes of the mountain. Frankie swung along happily, glad of the day out.

'This is good,' she said. 'I feel in the mood to conquer the Matterhorn today.'

'You're tied too much to Riverdale. Young Julie ought to give a hand sometimes. What's she going to do with herself now she's left school?'

'She only left last week. Doesn't seem to have any plans beyond Don Birchington.'

'That's still going strong?'

'As far as I know. She's hardly ever in, and when she is she doesn't confide in me. She's away this weekend, staying with a school-friend, she says. If I were Caroline, I'd be worried, but she seems to think it's all right to give Julie her head.'

'I guess Julie's got a cool enough head. I feel a bit sorry for the kid. She's probably asked for bread and got stones in the past, too. But I'd better not get on to her upbringing or I shall be treading on the area we have to rope off.'

'And I don't intend to let anything spoil this day. If only the weather stays like this, visibility should be good on top. How long do you reckon it will take us?'

'About two hours to get up. One hour down. That's taking it briskly.'

The first part of their climb was easy going along a grassy path with outcrops of rock. They had left the valley behind, and it was open walking now with what looked like a vertical face of shaly rock ahead of them.

'Not so bad as it looks,' said Rolf.

Frankie had no breath for speech, however, during the steep climb up that section. When they came out on to a less steep area of sparse grass above, they stopped for a short rest. Frankie was puffing and her calves ached, but Rolf would not let her linger long.

'We'll do our resting on the way back,' he said. 'You'll only lose rhythm and stiffen up if you stop now.'

The grass soon disappeared and they were on loose stone and shale again. There was no clear path, but the way was marked by cairns. The last stretch was very steep, and Frankie was glad of Rolf's helping hand now and again. Then they were on the ridge.

'Look,' he said, turning her round to look south, and she exclaimed with delight when she saw spread out below them the whole grand stretch of Cardigan Bay from the Lleyn Peninsula to St. David's Head, while to the north lay the ranges of the high Welsh mountains. The sun had come out between the white cumulus clouds that moved across the sky like sheep, and the landscape all around them was picked out clear and sharp. The wind was fierce up there, and Rolf held her shoulders and drew her against him as a sudden gust made her stagger.

'How beautiful!' she exclaimed.

'All the kingdoms of the world, and the glory of them,' quoted Rolf.

They remained there for some minutes in silence. Moved by the grandeur of the landscape, conscious of Rolf's firm support behind her, she knew that this was something she would never forget. This man. This moment in time. She turned and looked up at him, and when his dark eyes met hers knew that something had passed between them, some shared glory, some commitment.

Then two more climbers appeared below them, plodding up between the cairns, and the spell was broken. The ridge on which they were standing had been approached on a gradual contour from the side they had climbed, but on the other side it fell away precipitously and just below the summit on this precipitous side was a large lake. As they stood looking down at this, the sun vanished behind another pile of white cloud and the wind felt cold. They started down as the ascending party reached the summit, and kept up a smart pace.

'I'm glad the weather was so good for the view,' said Rolf. 'Often it's obscured by cloud or mist. Couldn't have been better this time. I don't think I've ever seen it so crystal clear. Aftermath of yesterday's rain, I suppose.'

They delayed eating their lunch until they had reached a green oasis on the bank of the stream through the valley. Here, protected from the wind, warmed by the sun, they attacked their lunch with zest, and afterwards lounged back in the grass, using Frankie's raincoat as a ground sheet, in a state of lazy content.

'This is a lovely country,' said Frankie dreamily, gazing at the sky through a twinkling canopy of silver birch leaves. 'No wonder your father came back to it.'

'The valleys and mountains he knew as a boy. I suppose any country you love in childhood pulls you back again. With me it's Mallorca.'

'And you, with Welsh blood in your veins! What would your Uncle Elwyn say?'

'Oh, I have my allegiance to Wales. I like the high places, but I find the valleys and the too frequent rain a bit oppressive. This has never seemed a happy country to me, but then the kind of life you experience in a place colours your opinion of it. Here, I often feel I'm smothered. I can't breathe. Caught in a web.'

'And in Mallorca?'

'The sunshine and laughter and freedom I had there when I was a kid still put a rosy light over the island for me. Now its coastline is being built up and overrun with summer tourists, but inland it's still the same. You go back centuries in the mountain villages.'

'Your grandmother lives inland?'

'Yes. They've an estate in the foothills. Grow almond trees and oranges. Almonds are the main crop there. There are millions of almond trees in Mallorca. You should see it at the end of January when the trees are in bloom.'

'Tell me about it, Rolf. You reveal so little of your life. Tell me about your boyhood there.'

'I only lived there for a year, but we spent a lot of holidays there as well. And I've been back as often as I could. Why should I bore you with it, though? Go for yourself one day and see. But go in January or February, before the tourists arrive. The weather's delightful then. Cool, but sunny. Avoid December and early January, when the rains come.'

'I'm not bored with hearing about your life. You're too reserved, Rolf. I want to know.'

'Why?'

'Because to know about the past is to understand the present better.'

'True enough.'

He talked to her then about Mallorca, its people and customs. And with a little prodding, he went on to talk about the holidays he had spent across the water from Mallorca in Andalusia.

'There are similarities between Southern Spain and Mallorca, of course, but the mainland is wilder, harsher, just as beautiful and more challenging,' he said.

'These holidays in Andalusia. On your own?'

'A few with Miguel. Often on my own.'

A loner, she thought, her eyes on his lean brown hand on the grass beside hers. Was he born a loner, or, as his father seemed to hint, had circumstances turned him into one?

'And what about you?' he asked lazily, putting his hand on hers. 'You investigate me, but say little of your life before you came here. Brothers? Sisters?'

A little disconcerted by this sudden change of direction, Frankie told him about her sister. Any mention of Nick might lead to enquiries about where he lived or what he did. She concentrated on Jenny and went on to Grandma Rainwood, a matriarch who was good for several amusing anecdotes.

Some time, she thought, she would have to tell him about Nick. She was sure Caroline exaggerated the bad effect this would have. If his father had some phobia about anything remotely connected with the press, he need not be told. But Rolf was surely not as unreasonably biassed as his father, although Caroline had maintained that he was. But today, in the unexpected state of happiness that had arisen between them, was not the day to introduce any controversy. It would mean bringing Caroline into it again, and that subject opened up a gulf between them immediately. The bridge between her and Rolf had to be strengthened before subjecting it to any strain.

'She sounds a rare character, your Grandma Rainwood,' he said. 'Marvellous, the spunk so many of that generation seem to have. Today we seem to come in a more sloppy mould.'

'And anyone less sloppy than you, my lord, I never came across.'

'Perhaps sloppy was the wrong word. Uncertain. Less sure of our standards. And am I your lord?' he asked with a gleam in his eyes as he ruffled her short hair.

'Lordly, anyway.'

'And that riles you?'

'Sometimes. More tolerance would make things easier.'

'I'm in a situation which is a bit fraying, Frankie.'

'In what way? Apart from family differences, which we won't go into.'

'And which are at the root of it. If I asked you to give up your job at Riverdale and get a job in Marlbury, perhaps with our company, I suppose you'd refuse.'

'Yes. I couldn't let Caroline or your father down at this stage. And why on earth should I?'

'Because you can't run with the hare and hunt with the hounds, my dear.'

'I won't believe that just because you and Caroline don't get on, it need affect us.'

'It means there must always be that piece of no-man's-land between us.'

'Aren't you forgetting your father? He needs me now.'

'Yes, of course. You've done a lot to make his life more bearable, and heaven knows I wouldn't want to deprive him of that. Forget it. My life seems fated to be entangled by circumstances not of my making and which I can't cut through.'

'Rolf, you must know that my job at Riverdale is only temporary,' she said gently.

'Yes. My father's losing ground. I had a word with the doctor the other day. He doesn't give him more than a few months. At least, that's what I gathered from his ifs and buts and professional look-on-the-bright side. Since my father doesn't see death as an enemy, such false optimism is a bit wasted on him.'

'I've grown very fond of him.'

Rolf put his arm round her shoulders and drew her closer.

'One day, Frankie, we'll stand in the clear, accountable only to each other. Until then, there's not much I can say or do.'

'What about your work? Doesn't that satisfy you, either?'

'It's not what I trained for. I spend far too much time on the administrative side, too little on the creative. I'd never any intention of going into the building trade. I planned to go into practice as an architect as soon as I'd qualified and got the necessary experience in a professional firm. But after I'd had a few years with a firm of architects in London, my father had the stroke, and asked me to come back and take over his job in the business just so that I could be near him for what he thought would be at best the last year of his life. I couldn't refuse and leave him helpless and confined to Riverdale. That was five years ago.'

'But you are using your professional qualifications there.'

'Up to a point. It's stereotyped work, though. Housing estates where cost is the be-all and end-all. My uncles are good business men, but not inclined to pander to architectural flights of fancy. We've had our fights. Now I go along with them, biding my time, but I'm looking forward to the day when I can be a professional man and not a business man, have some creative scope and be in a position to quarrel more easily with builders over the quality of materials. Where I am, I'm ham-strung.'

'Does that mean going back to London?'

'Yes. As a matter of fact, a friend of mine wants me to go into partnership with him. He's a good architect with a growing practice. I shall join him when I'm free.'

She was beginning to understand now why he so often conveyed an impression of bottled-up impatience. A man involved with his family and yet not of them. A strong will frustrated, making him more hard and intolerant than was comfortable. Yet he had made the sacrifice for his father and was unstinting in his devotion. Gradually, she was getting to know the reserved and complex man who was Rolf Falkland.

'The Falklands will be sorry to lose you.'

'I shall act for them if they want me. They're nice folk, the Mynelly lot. Rabidly Welsh. It's rumoured that Uncle Lloyd has been out painting over all the English signposts with green paint, substituting Welsh names where there's space. I wouldn't put it past him, either. The fact that my knowledge of the Welsh language is a bit sketchy is a sore point. Boy, you should speak the tongue of your fathers,' concluded Rolf in Lloyd's lilting Welsh voice.

'I like them, too. Poor Rolf. Pulled in so many different directions.'

'Mmm. Another one now, too.' He sat up and leaned over her, one arm on either side. 'You do see, Frankie, that the board is a bit messed up. Some time, perhaps, we can get it clear. You want that?'

'Yes.'

'So do I. For the time being, it's stalemate, though.'

'Don't remind me of that dreadful game, chess. My brain gets worn out trying to plot about six moves ahead.'

He laughed and stood up, holding out his hands.

'Come on. Time we got moving. You look far too tempting there for my peace of mind.'

He pulled her to her feet and removed a dead leaf from her hair. His face wore a gentle expression she had never seen there before. But he looked troubled, too, she thought.

'Thank you for a lovely day, Rolf. One I shall always remember.'

'And so shall I. If I were you, I wouldn't enthuse too much to Caroline.'

'I wish I could mend this breach.'

'As well think you could beat my father at chess. One day, Frankie, you'll have to make a choice. I can't make it for you. I've said it before, and I'll say it again. There can be no compromise here.'

His face was austere now, unyielding. The sun had gone in behind a cloud and she shivered. Her legs felt stiff as they started back along the path by the stream. For the rest of the way, Rolf kept the conversation to impersonal matters as though nothing had happened between them, but she knew that up there on the summit of Cader a link had been forged and that it was the most important thing that had ever happened to her. And no amount of reminders to herself of the dangers of hypnosis, of the power Rolf wielded, of much that was daunting in his make-up, could weaken the conviction that now, for better or for worse, Rolf Falkland mattered in her life. She had climbed a mountain and felt the touch of glory.

Rolf had left the car where the track emerged into a lane, and they were both quiet on the drive back to Riverdale. He spent the evening with his father. Frankie walked out to the car with him when he left. Caroline had gone to bed early with a book, to Frankie's relief, for she had found it difficult to talk casually about the day's expedition.

'Tired?' he asked.

'Still have my head in the stars no matter how my legs feel.'

'You did well. I can see you'd be a good partner in the high hills.'

'My life's been too confined. I'm ready for more exploration.'

'We'll go and see that almond blossom together one day,' he

said, and laid a hand on her shoulder briefly before getting into the car.

She watched until the rear lights disappeared round a bend in the drive. Until this day, she had not suspected a poetic streak in Rolf. She went to bed and dreamed of almond blossom and mountains and a wide, raging river that threatened to drown her.

11
Julie

FOR the next few weeks, Frankie was confined to the house more than usual by wet weather that set in at the beginning of August, so that when towards the end of the month a dry if overcast day presented itself for a change, she decided to make the most of it and spend the day in the foothills. With a packet of sandwiches in her raincoat pocket, she set off across the garden, which was the shortest cut to the river path on which her walk started. The growth in the garden during the past few weeks had been phenomenal, and the path through the belt of shrubs which she had cut back only a month or two ago was already partially blocked again. Before she could get the wheel-chair through here, she would have to do some clearing. When she came out to the little garden she had made, evidence of recent neglect was all too apparent. The pinks were a sodden mess of dead brown flowers, and ragwort and groundsel had taken over the petunias she had bedded out behind the pinks. She was aghast at what could happen in a garden in a few short weeks of neglect. Her determination that Trevor Falkland should have at least one piece of well-kept garden to sit in seemed to be fighting a losing battle. Gardening, she though pessimistically, was evidently a hobby which demanded almost daily effort to thwart nature's jungle, especially when you had made your small oasis in the midst of weed-infested acres from which weed seeds in their thousands drifted in the wind.

She sat down on the seat, aware of a sore throat and a lassitude which suggested that she had caught the cold from which Julie was only just recovering. Perhaps she would change her mind about the walk and do a little work in the garden instead. Trevor Falkland, too, had been shut up by the wet weather, and she would like to bring him here at the first opportunity, but in this state her little plot shamed her. She lingered on the seat, impatient with her tiredness but unwilling to move. Mrs. Filey had been unwell during the past week and there had been a lot of fetching and carrying to do. It was Caroline, home this weekend, who had urged Frankie to take the day off. Next week, she was taking her mother to the south coast for a fortnight's holiday. It was a pity, thought Frankie, that on her first free day for some time, she should feel below par; such a rare experience with her that she felt almost indignant about it.

At last she roused herself to go back to the house to change into her gardening slacks. In the hall, hearing Caroline's laughter from the sitting-room, she put her head round the door to tell her of her change of plan. Don Birchington, Julie and Caroline each had a glass of champagne in their hands.

'Congratulations, Don. And my blessings, Julie darling. I hope you'll both be very happy,' Caroline said, and they drank.

It was Julie who saw Frankie first. She put her left hand hastily behind her back and gave her mother a warning glance. Caroline turned and looked surprised to see Frankie.

'I thought you'd gone out for the day, dear.' She paused for a moment, then smiled gaily. 'But do come in and join our little secret celebration. These two have sprung a surprise on me. They're engaged.'

'Not quite a surprise, Mummy. I did tell you yesterday.'

'Fetch another champagne glass from the sideboard, Frankie.'

When she returned, Don filled her glass, and Caroline toasted them all over again. Frankie tried to hide her consternation. It was not her business to judge. Julie, flushed and excited, showed her the cluster of diamonds on her finger, while Don eyes his fiancée with a proprietary air of satisfaction. It was small wonder that the girl's head had been turned, thought Frankie, for flowers and presents had come in a steady flow from Don for weeks past. He took her out to smart restaurants, dances, night clubs. He had all the smooth assurance and sophistication calculated to impress any young girl. But he was twice Julie's age, and she had only just left school. How could Caroline be so pleased about it?

She explained her change of plan and was about to leave when Caroline said, 'You realise that this must be a secret engagement for the time being, Frankie, don't you? Trevor mustn't know. He's very old-fashioned and would think Julie too young, and I can't have him worried or upset. It would be dangerous for him. So it goes no further than we four for the time being.'

'I understand.'

'Be very careful, won't you? No unguarded remarks. Not to anybody. I know we can count on your co-operation.'

'Of course,' said Frankie quietly, and left them to go up to her room.

She had just pulled on a cotton sweater when there was a knock on her door and Caroline came in.

'Our turtle doves are going out to lunch in Marlbury and then drive to the coast to celebrate the occasion.' She sat down on the divan and crossed her legs with a friendly smile. 'I thought you seemed a little short of enthusiasm about the engagement, and that a chat might reassure you.'

'Well, it's none of my business, is it? I just feel that Don's too old for Julie. That she hasn't had time to look around.'

'But I married a man much older than myself. Some women need more of a parental element. Julie's following in my footsteps.'

Surely she couldn't think there was anything paternal about Don Birchington, thought Frankie. But her statement about her own marriage was unanswerable. The gap between Caroline and her husband was almost as large as that between Julie and Don.

'Do you like him?' asked Frankie bluntly.

'Yes. Well, a little brash, perhaps, for my taste, but good-hearted, devoted to Julie, and a successful man, able to look after her and give her a comfortable life. I'm relieved to think she'll be looked after so well.'

'But Mr. Falkland will have to know some time.'

'Of course. But we'll cross that bridge when we get to it. I could have wished that Julie had waited a little, perhaps, but she was eighteen last week. She's of an age to decide for herself. And if my husband got to know of it and made trouble, you know what Julie would do, don't you?'

'Yes. Of course, you're right.'

'So for all our sakes, Trevor's and the rest of us, he mustn't know, or suspect. That means extra care when you're with his relations. And particularly Rolf. He wouldn't be above making trouble. So we're responsible, you and I, for seeing that Trevor's health isn't threatened by the worry this could cause him.'

'I understand. I'll be careful.'

'Dear Frankie. It's such a help to me to have your support. It's not that Trevor hasn't Julie's happiness at heart. I wouldn't suggest that for a moment. But he's out of touch with the modern world, with young people. He sees Julie as a schoolgirl still. Doesn't realise that young people mature so much earlier now. He's so old-fashioned. I've told them they mustn't be in a hurry and they've agreed to keep it secret. I hope Julie takes good care of that ring. It must have cost Don a small fortune. I shall take out an insurance for it. Now I must go. I've one or two things to press ready for packing tomorrow. Are you good at packing, Frankie?'

'Reasonably.'

'I'm terrible. I wonder if you'd be an angel and do it for me tomorrow. I'll put everything out ready.'

'Of course. But I'm not holding myself out as the perfect packer.'

'You can't be as bad as I am. I do hope this weather improves. But the south coast should be an improvement on Wales for weather, anyway. It will do Mother so much good to be able to rest in the sun. The hotel has a sheltered terrace and a lovely garden. It's the first time I've been able to persuade her to come away for years. It does mean an effort, poor dear. But worth while.'

Frankie, chopping away at the dead pinks, had reluctantly to admit that Caroline had reason on her side in her attitude to Julie's engagement. But that she should be so happy at the prospect was surprising. And once again she was put in the position of having to guard her tongue with Rolf. Increasingly it was becoming difficult to run with the hare and hunt with the hounds, as he had warned her. And yet, what else could she do? She was fond of Caroline, who had been generous and kind to her. And her wish to guard her husband from all worry deserved support. And, all else apart, Caroline was her employer and had a right to expect her loyalty. But Rolf was a perceptive person, quick to sense when she was holding back. And she was not skilful at holding back, anyway. Now there was another topic that must be skirted; another patch of no-man's-land between them.

By the Monday morning, when Caroline was due to leave, Frankie's cold was streaming and Mrs. Filey's gastritis was so severe that Caroline asked Frankie to telephone for the doctor.

'I've no patience with her stubborn refusal to see a doctor,' said Caroline. 'He would have given her some medicine last week that would have relieved the trouble quite quickly. She's had it before, and always we've had to wait until it reached this stage before calling him.'

'And even now she'd prefer some herbal concoction of her own making,' said Frankie. 'She makes a vile brew of several herbs that grow in odd corners of the garden and swears it cures everything. She tried to get me to take some for this cold. It was revolting.'

'My dear, don't let her give you gastritis as well. I'm sure it's some of these country remedies that cause the trouble. At one time she tried to persuade Trevor to take some. I soon put a stop to that. But it is inconvenient, having her laid up now. I hate leaving you to cope with it all, dear, but I can't postpone this holiday, and nor can Mother travel down on her own.'

'Of course not. Don't worry. I can manage.'

'And you with a bad cold, too. I'm so sorry.'

'I always throw colds off quickly. That sounds like Jim Davis.'

It was the diminutive driver of the hired car, who hailed Caroline cheerfully. He was like a little wizened gnome, and nobody could guess at his age. He picked up Caroline's two large suitcases and tried to gather up the small one, too, but Frankie forestalled him. Following him out to the car, she could see that it was as much as he could do to carry them, but he waved aside her offer to help.

'And leave a little lady like you to carry one? What would I be thinking about, then?'

'You're so kind, Jim. Now are you sure you can manage?' said Caroline, following them down the steps.

He stowed the cases away and helped Caroline into the car as though handling royalty. Everybody was glad to be of service to Caroline's fragile beauty, thought Frankie as she waved them off.

There were times during the following week when Frankie wished she had a fragile beauty to appeal to a stalwart helper, for her cold was unusually severe and prolonged, and Mrs. Filey had to remain in bed the whole week. Coping with meals for both invalids, helped half-heartedly and rarely by Julie, she felt exhausted by the end of the first week of Caroline's absence. It was not so much the chores, she thought, as the cough which kept her awake for much of the night.

On the Sunday evening Rolf took a hand, and being Rolf, would brook no argument.

'Go to bed for a couple of days,' he said. 'I'll get Mrs. Lewis to come here and take over. She's the body who does for me. A decent, willing woman. My father knows her, and so does Mrs. Filey.'

'How do you know she can come?' croaked Frankie.

'Because she'll come here instead of coming to me. I'll drop in on my way home tonight and tell her. Now, off to bed with you. I'll finish here.'

He had picked up the tea-cloth and was attacking the stack of dishes Frankie had washed when he heard the front door close.

'Julie,' he called. 'Here.'

She came in, looking cool and pretty in a pale green linen suit.

'I'm sending Frankie off to bed for a couple of days. She's not fit to be about. I'm arranging for Mrs. Lewis to come in tomorrow. Meanwhile, you take over. And you can start now,' he said curtly, handing her the tea-cloth.

She opened her mouth to protest, then said sulkily, 'I must change my shoes first. I'm tired and my feet ache.'

'Too bad. You'll feel better when you get out of those stilts. And don't be long. I'm just going to make a hot toddy for Frankie and you can take it up.'

Julie looked furious, and Frankie left them to fight it out, having no doubt about who the victor would be. She felt too weak just then to be drawn into it. Julie brought in the glass of toddy with a tight-lipped expression of martyrdom, and echoed Frankie's 'Goodnight' in a cold voice before she went. Frankie sighed, sipping the hot drink and drawing comfort from the welcome support of her bed, thinking that she would never understand Julie. The girl revealed so little, and was surprisingly cool and collected for such a young girl. She wondered whether that was the reason she attracted Don Birchington. Perhaps that very coolness was a challenge to him. A pretty snow maiden to be melted and possessed. And if he had found her melting point, Frankie hadn't, and never would, it seemed.

After a couple of days in bed, her natural resilence came to her aid and, with Mrs. Filey still shaky but up and about, things were almost back to normal by the end of that second week of Caroline's absence. On the Friday night she was listening to a concert on the radio in her room when Julie came in, looking bothered.

'Frankie, something awful's happened. I need your help.'

Frankie switched off the radio and Julie went on, 'When I came in tonight, my father caught me in the hall and asked me to come into his study. He'd got some travel brochures he wanted to show me. Now that I've left school, he thinks it would be nice for me to have a holiday abroad. With Caroline, of course. But we'd go through the brochures together and he'd advise me.'

'A kind thought.'

'I'd got my engagement ring on and hadn't a pocket or a bag to slip in into. When I said I'd go and tidy my hair, he said not to worry and would I wheel him back to his study. He wanted to talk about it now. You know what he's like in that tetchy mood. I kept my left hand hidden as well as I could but I knew it would be impossible to hide it from him once we started leafing over those brochures.'

'And so?'

'Well, he'd got his desk drawer open. The top one. He'd been sorting out some papers, I think. In a panic, behind my back, I slipped off the ring and dropped it in the drawer, and scuffled some papers over it. I thought I could wait until he went to bed, and then get it back. Oh, I know it wasn't a very good plan, but it was all I could think of on the spur of the moment.'

'And he hasn't gone to bed yet?'

'No. He said he'd still got a few bills to sort out when I asked him if I could wheel him into his bedroom. But he'd shut the drawer. Does he keep it locked, that one?'

'Not as a rule. He keeps stamps and bills and household papers in it.'

'Well, you usually go in about now to see if he wants anything, don't you? Could you get the ring back? It will be easy if he's in his bedroom. If not, you can make some excuse and get it, can't you? I'm never in there. It will look odd if I go back and start fishing around. But you're his secretary. And I'm scared of him.'

'My dear Julie, there's nothing to be scared of. Your father's a kind man.'

'But he mustn't know about my engagement. Oh, if only Caroline were here! She'd know what to do. She could say it was hers. But she won't be back until Monday, and he's almost bound to go to that drawer and find it before then. And how can we explain it?'

'This is always liable to happen if you wear it, Julie.'

'I only wear it when I'm out with Don. After all, if a man gives a girl an expensive ring, he expects to see it on her finger

Julie

when they're together. In any normal house there wouldn't be all this trouble,' she ended irritably.

'Well, I'll see what I can do,' said Frankie, not liking her task. 'But do be more careful. Take the ring off before you come into the house. You usually have a handbag with you, don't you?'

'Yes. But I left it in the car tonight. I forgot it. Just my luck, as things turned out. But it should be simple enough for you to get it back, Frankie,' she coaxed. 'I daren't rouse his suspicions. Caroline would be furious, and heaven knows what would happen. Anyone would think I was committing a crime, getting engaged.'

'Are you really happy about it, Julie?'

She opened her eyes wide as she looked at Frankie.

'Happy? Of course I am. Why should I get engaged otherwise?'

'Don's so much older than you.'

'I don't like young men. They're messy and boring and haven't an idea in their heads. Their notion of marriage is just having someone to wash and cook for them and look after the baby. At least, that's what they're like round here. And I don't intend to spend my life in this dull place. Don can show me the world. We'll have a good time together. Dad's plan for a nice little holiday abroad with Caroline which was meant to impress and thrill me fell a bit flat, I'm afraid. I shall be going abroad, but it will be to Paris and Nice and the Caribbean, and it won't be with my mother. Not that Caroline isn't a good sport. But a man's a better escort.'

'Marriage is for a long time. Do you love him?'

Julie smiled a superior little smile that made Frankie want to spank her.

'We get on splendidly. But let's not discuss that. If my father's not to throw a fit on us, we've got to get that ring.'

'Well, I must say that leaving it in his desk wasn't the brightest of ideas.'

'I was in a panic, I tell you. There wasn't time to think up anything better. You've never seen him in a rage. I did, once. It frightened me. That ugly face, looking like murder. I hate violent people,' said Julie, shuddering.

It was true, thought Frankie, that the girl did have an inexplicable fear of her father, but for this Caroline bore some responsibility. Her attitude of keeping them apart for fear of trouble, her over-protectiveness, seemed to indicate that her husband was a tyrant, which Frankie knew was false. But perhaps there was a hint of the same smouldering intensity of feeling in the father that she sensed in Rolf, and that could be daunting. In the older man, though, all passion was now spent, she was sure. She spoke briskly.

'You'd better wait here. I'll go and see what the position is.'

When she knocked at the study door, there was no reply. She went in. The room was in darkness but a light shone from the bedroom.

'Do you want anything more tonight, Mr. Falkland?' she called.

'Come in, Frankie I've dropped my sticks. I wonder if you'd pick them up and put them handy for me.'

She put them where he could reach them from his chair. He was brooding over the chess board on the bedside table.

'Would you like anything to drink before you go to bed?'

'No, thank you dear. It doesn't seem as though Rolf will look in tonight. I'll just spend a little while plotting his downfall before I close down. We left this game at a very interesting stage. Very interesting. I think I can see a possible checkmate in sight, though.'

She smiled and left him, closing the door behind her. She hesitated in front of the desk, annoyed with Julie for putting her in this position. But she could see no good reason for allowing Trevor Falkland to be upset and worried by a selfish, calculating young person like Julie, who would certainly take things into her own hands if he intervened. The drawer was unlocked. She pushed aside the papers but could not see the ring. In the end, she had most of the contents of the drawer out before she spied it in the corner. She slipped it into the pocket of her dress and was putting the papers back when Rolf's voice sent her spinning round.

'Looking for something, Frankie?'

'Oh, it's you.' She recovered herself rapidly. 'Hullo, Rolf. Yes, I just wanted a stamp. We seem to be out of them.'

He looked at her closely, then said, 'Perhaps I can oblige.' He took out his wallet. 'Sorry. No go. I rely too much on the office. Anything urgent?'

'No. It can wait until I'm next in the village. Your father's just working out how he can checkmate you. He'd given you up for tonight.'

'Yes. I got held up. You're looking better.'

'I'm quite fit again now, thanks.'

'You've left this out,' he said, picking up a letter which had slipped on to the leather chair in front of the desk. He put it back in the drawer, then picked up the bunch of keys which Frankie had not noticed at the back of the desk behind the calendar. He tossed them in his hand thoughtfully.

'Does the old man usually leave these keys lying about?'

'No. He must have overlooked them tonight. He's been doing some household accounts.'

'I'll give them to him.'

Frankie, the ring burning a hole in her pocket, said with a lightness which she did not feel, 'I'll leave you to wriggle out of that checkmate, then.'

Julie looked immensely relieved when Frankie handed her the ring.

'Thanks a lot. I'll be more careful in future, I promise. That was Rolf I heard downstairs, I suppose.'

'Yes. He's with his father now.'

'He didn't see the ring?'

'No.'

Julie let out a puff of relief.

'Thank goodness for that. He'd be as bad as Father. Perhaps worse. Detestable, bossy creature. Coming in and out of Riverdale as though he owns it. He could be very nasty I know. How you could spend a day out with him I can't imagine, though Caroline said you did the other week.'

'We climbed Cader Idris.'

'What for?'

'The view at the top.'

'Well, if I were you, I wouldn't fraternise with him. Of course he's attractive in a way. I can see that. But dangerous. Why don't you make more use of Barry? He's much nicer, and I think he's a bit smitten with you. He's the nicest of that Falkland crowd. You must find it awfully dull here. He'd cheer things up a bit for you.'

'I'll bear it in mind,' said Frankie solemnly.

Julie stared at her suspiciously. She had no sense of humour. Then she shrugged her shoulders.

'Well, thanks, anyway, for getting back my ring and saving a show-down. Isn't it a beauty?' she added, flashing the diamonds in the light of the standard lamp.

In her petal-pink sheath dress, slender as a reed, her fair hair smooth and shining, she looked so pretty and untouched as she stood there, admiring the ring.

12
Problems

THE grass outside the study window was covered with yellow and brown leaves from the sycamore and chestnut trees nearby, and more were dropping as wind and rain beat through the branches. After a fine October, winter seemed suddenly to be at the door.

'You look pensive, my dear. Anything wrong?' asked Trevor Falkland from the desk.

Frankie turned and sighed.

'Just autumnal blues.'

'Well, there's only one letter I'd like you to do for me this morning, so come and share this pot of coffee with me and we'll see if I can cheer you up. You cheer me up so often, it's time I tried to repay you in the same coin. Now sit in the armchair there, and I'll do the honours.'

He poured out a cup of coffee and handed it to her. His face looked grey and drawn, but the dark eyes that studied her looked sympathetic.

'Don't indulge my mood. I've no good reason for it and must snap out of it. I don't deserve indulgence,' she said.

'That's a matter of opinion. Seriously, you've looked peaky lately. I've thought you seemed unhappy.'

'Well, a little troubled perhaps."

'Can't you tell me?'

'You have so many troubles of your own.'

'And so people shut me out of theirs. What does that make me? A useless onlooker?'

'No. Never,' she protested quickly. 'Your companionship is something I value very much. It's no longer just a duty. You must know that by now.'

'Thank you, Frankie. Yes, we've made contact, I think. Forgive me, my dear. I don't mean to pry. But is it Rolf? You and he have seemed . . . not quite in harmony lately. And yet I thought you were good friends before. Is there any trouble I might be able to lift? I know my son better than anybody, after all.'

'It's not really anything tangible. Just that I feel . . . well, it's absurd, but I feel that he doesn't quite trust me. It's this lack of trust in Rolf that I find disturbing. It seems to put a barrier between us.'

'He is essentially a reserved man. Doesn't easily let his defences down. That's because he learned the need for armour at a very early age. But you and he, I thought, were getting to understand each other rather well.'

'I like him so much, but there's a lot I don't understand about him and that scares me a little. Underneath, I feel he's a bit volcanic,' she added with a rueful little smile.

'You can cope with that, I'm sure. He's played a lone hand too long. I'd like to see him marry. The right woman could work wonders for him, as his mother did for me. He needs warmth in his life. I wouldn't want him to grow harder and more sceptical about life as the years go by, and I fear that could happen. In one way or another, he's been fighting adverse circumstances for most of his life. And that's a toughening experience, Frankie. I'd like him to experience the gentler side of life some time. Life isn't all a battle, though sometimes it seems so.'

'Well, he's certainly an effective fighter.'

'And could be an equally effective lover, given the opportunity. He may seem hard, but he's not a cold man.'

'No. That I've realised. We shall sort things out between us, I expect,' she added cheerfully.

'And hope?'

Her eyes met his gravely as she said, 'Yes, I hope so.'

'And so do I.'

She was to remember that little exchange later on, but just then was gripped by a pessimistic feeling that she would never understand Rolf. Since the incident with the ring, there had been a cloud between them. Nothing tangible, but the sense of intimacy had gone. But always, she knew, it came back to her loyalty to Caroline. There was the rock on which they split. She could see no good reason for his hostility and suspicion. The choice he wanted to force on her was not necessary. But more and more she felt her foothold slipping in this house of divisions, so that it was with a feeling of relief that she looked forward to going home at the end of that week for a brief holiday, her first since taking on this job. It would be good to see Nick again and hear the family news.

'You do yourself very well, Nick,' said Frankie, lying back in the armchair and stretching her toes to the fire. 'I like your flat.'

'Mmm. It's not bad.'

'And your Mrs. Green bakes jolly good cakes,' she said, biting into her second.

'I wish she wouldn't. I haven't a sweet tooth myself, but the old dear thinks I need building up and since I falsely told her how much I enjoyed her cakes the first time she brought me some as a surprise, she brings them regularly. That's what comes of being a hypocrite.'

'Well, you couldn't hurt her feelings. I expect she sees you as the ideal son she never had. Little does she know of the cool sceptic under that charming surface. Another cup of tea?'

'Please.' Nick lit a cigarette and eyed her. 'You're looking a bit thin. Are they running you off your feet down in wild Wales?'

'I'm kept pretty busy. Caroline's away a lot. Her mother is a great worry to her.'

'I saw her the other day. Going into a block of flats in Kensington.'

'Did she see you?'

'No. I was on the other side of the road with a friend. She was carrying an enormous bunch of yellow chrysanthemums and from where I stood, would have been taken for an extremely pretty girl in her twenties, except that she was so much better groomed than most girls I see around. Is that where her mother lives?'

'Kensington? I'm not sure that Caroline's ever mentioned it, but I know her mother lives in London.'

'Rather nice flats. I had my eye on one there, but it was too expensive for me. It's the block we passed on the way to the Albert Hall when I took you to that Berlioz concert about a year ago. You were taken with that little piece of sculpture on the lawn in the front. Remember?'

'Vaguely. What a memory you've got for detail, Nick!'

'My writer's eye,' he said, grinning. 'Sorry I haven't been able to see you before, but I wanted to do this research at Carisbrooke, and time was pressing. Pity you can't stay longer.'

'I've enjoyed my few days, but I'm quite ready to go back now. I've done my duty by the family and been brought up to date by Grandma.'

'What's the position at Riverdale? How is the old man?'

'Failing, I'm afraid. Even in the ten months I've been there, he's lost a lot of ground. He's a stoic, though. Never complains. I sometimes wonder whether Caroline realises, but then she's wearing herself out commuting between London and Wales, and gave me a fright last week when she collapsed and had to go to bed for a couple of days. Said it was nothing. Her blood pressure's a bit above normal. But I don't want another invalid on my hands.'

'She looked fit enough when I saw her. Seems rather a depressing job I introduced you to. Are you sure you want to carry on?'

'I'm happy down there. I like Mr. Falkland so much, and Caroline's very kind and generous to me. They need me. And it's good to be needed.'

'And the son? I rather gathered, reading between the lines of your last letter, that he appeared in a better light on top of a mountain than down in the valley,' said Nick in his most marked ironic drawl.

'A much better light. But still a prickly proposition,' said Frankie carefully, studying her tea.

'Well, as a sleuth you're very disappointing, but if you're getting on the soft side of Rolf, perhaps I can still hope. He might know more about his father than Caroline does. After all, he must have been on the scene when his father was a writer.'

'He's as tight as a clam about the past. I only know that to his father, it's very bitter. But that may have nothing to do with his writing. He told me once that he'd spoiled Rolf's life. He's full of self-reproach, but what for, I can't imagine. He's such a good man.'

'Yes, I think that shows in his books. What's behind it all? Must be something.'

'Oh, I don't know. Who doesn't have regrets about the past? Your writer's imagination is too active in this case, I'm sure.'

'I just can't believe that a man with that talent could stop writing.'

'Perhaps his imagination dried up. Perhaps it was all too much of a grind. He had a wife and son to support, and from what you tell me, writers don't earn much money.'

'But it's a compulsion, to use that sort of creative talent. Anyway, keep your eyes and ears open, Frankie. I always like to get to the bottom of anything that puzzles me. Any crumbs of enlightenment will be welcome. I'd still like to write that article on him, but I haven't enough to go on.'

'He hates publicity. You wouldn't do it without his consent, would you?'

'No. But there's the future, when it can't worry him.'

'I should feel bound by his wishes. Always,' said Frankie firmly.

'All right. But just for my own private satisfaction, I'd like to know more about a writer whose work I admire so much. He shouldn't be allowed to go into oblivion.'

'That's what he wants, and it's his life.'

'Once you publish your work, it's no longer yours. And my interest is based on admiration, nothing else, Frankie.'

'I'd like to read those books some time.'

'You shall. What about taking one back with you, all excited about having discovered a book by Trevor Falkland, and asking him if it's his? Then he might tell you about it.'

'I only once ever brought up the subject of writing. I was reading the latest book by that friend of Jenny's, Martin Brayke. I lent it to Mr. Falkland and told him I'd met the author. I asked him whether he thought writing was a good career these days, because Martin seemed to be finding it hard going.'

'And?' prompted Nick as she hesitated.

'He closed up immediately. Said he didn't think it had ever been easy, but he really knew little about it. Then he started talking about something else. I've never tried again.'

'And Rolf? He's never let on anything about his father having once been a writer?'

'Never. He told me that his father had once had a personal tragedy when the press showed up at their worst, and that ever since then, any publicity was abhorrent to him. But I wrote and told you about that. It's no use, Nick. I can't pry into the past. That tragedy probably has nothing to do with Mr. Falkland's early career as a writer, but it bars any probing into the past. One day, perhaps, Rolf will tell me. But there's got to be a lot more trust between us before he will. And I wouldn't distress Mr. Falkland, or add the smallest worry to the burdens he already carries, for all the books in the world.'

'I see your point. And I certainly wouldn't want to put you in an ambiguous situation.'

'I'm in that already, but that's because of Caroline, and Rolf's unreasonable hostility to her. I still live in hope of thawing the ice between them, though.'

'Crusading again?'

'I knew you'd say that. But I must try.'

'Because?'

'Because it gets between Rolf and me.'

'And that matters?'

'Yes.'

'I see. Well, call on me if you need any help. And if you should come across anything that throws light on Trevor Falkland's writing career which your conscience will allow you to pass on, I promise to treat it in the strictest confidence and not use it without full permission from all parties. It's just that unanswered questions nag at me like the last unsolved word in a crossword puzzle.'

'If I can put that questing mind of yours to rest, I'll do so. But, believe me, there are lots of stiff bolts at Riverdale, and I don't intend to bruise my hands trying to force them.'

'An apt metaphor,' said Nick approvingly. 'You're coming on.'

'Big brother. What about your affairs? You dissect mine, but keep pretty close about yours, I notice. No romance? No ambitions about to be fulfilled?'

'I don't go in for romance, only harmless diversions now and again. And if by ambitions, you mean have I a book coasting round those many publishers who seem unable to discern my talent, the answer is that my latest, a brilliant survey of the literary scene of Tennyson's day, is in the final stages of revision and will start its rounds before the year is out.'

'Hence the visit to Carisbrooke.'

'As I said just now, you're coming on.'

'Well, the best of luck to it. Now if I'm to catch that train, I'd better think about moving.'

'You wouldn't like to take a bag of cakes with you to eat on the way, I suppose?'

'Anything to oblige. I might be glad of them before I'm back.'

Nick drove her to Paddington and supplied her with magazines but refused to see the train out.

'Last minute platitudes a waste of time,' he said, with his quirky smile. 'Take care of yourself, my dear, and curb your crusading zeal if you can. You'll get no thanks for it. So long.'

She leaned out of the window and watched his slim figure and fair head weave down the platform. He didn't turn. Nice Nick, she thought as she settled down in the corner of the carriage with her magazine.

13
Crisis

FROST had put a white lace trimming on all the trees and bushes in the hedgerow, and in the winter sunshine the mountains stood out with beautiful clarity against a pale blue sky. Well muffled-up, Frankie enjoyed her cycle ride to Rolf's cottage, and looked forward with eager curiosity to breaking into his hermitage with the perfectly legitimate excuse of bearing a document from his father for which he was waiting. Rolf, busy on a housing project for the firm that Saturday and off to Mallorca the next morning, would be unable to get to Riverdale, and so Frankie had been asked to act as messenger.

Passing the road junction that had been the scene of their near accident, she thought that, in a way, their whole relationship had been a bit like that. Near misses, when their friendship seemed doomed to split, followed by the warmth of belonging; then the cracks opening up again, to be bridged once more by that commitment to each other which neither of them voiced but which was there all the time.

The cottage looked cheerful and inviting in the sunshine, its mellow bricks and weathered tiled roof in harmony with the landscape of woods and meadows behind it. Smoke curled up lazily from a chimney-pot, and two starlings sat near by, chattering, their feathers glossy and shot with metallic shades of bronze and green in the sun. The windows were small and deeply eaved. The porch was festooned with a winter jasmine, just coming into bloom. She gave a vigorous tattoo with a lion-headed door-knocker. Rolf came to the door, and looked surprised to see her. He was wearing a heavy white Aran sweater with a green silk scarf tucked in at the neck, and dark cavalry twill slacks. His hair was ruffled and fell over his forehead, and the impression was altogether more relaxed than usual. It occurred to her then that it was for Riverdale he kept his armour on.

'Hullo,' she said cheerfully. 'Your father found this paper. He said you wanted it and asked me to bring it round.'

'Oh, thanks.' He put the envelope unopened into his pocket. 'Are you just passing or have you time to stop for a cup of coffee?'

'If I'm asked, I have time,' she said gravely.

Sitting in a large leather armchair in front of a log fire, she looked round the room with interest while Rolf went out to make some coffee. It was comfortable, masculine, with no frills, but warmed by the rich colours of the Persian carpet which covered the whole room. It was lined with bookshelves, and in the window a drawing board was set up with a high stool behind it. Frankie went across and studied the plan on the board. He had obviously just been working on it. She admired the printing on it, but could not make a visual picture of the sectional drawings.

She drifted over to the bookshelves, and then it struck her that Rolf might have copies of his father's books, and she scanned the shelves more carefully. She was only half way through, however, when he returned.

'A fine collection of books, Rolf.'

'Yes, I inherited a lot from my grandfather. We're a bookish lot. You make a bright addition to the room,' he added, eyeing her with approval.

She was wearing bottle-green slacks and the flame-coloured polo-necked sweater which Caroline had given her. Something in the gleam of his eyes confused her and she said hurriedly, 'I like slacks for cycling and gardening. They're so warm and comfortable. But I'm not tall enough to look well in them. Your friend Tracey looked stunning in them.'

'Think so? I prefer trimmer lines myself. And so does your friend Barry,' he said imperturbably.

'Tit for tat,' she said, smiling at him. 'I've interrupted your work, haven't I?'

'Yes. But you're a welcome interruption.'

'Thank you. How long are you going to be away?'

'Only until Thursday. It's my grandmother's seventy-fifth birthday on Monday and there's going to be a grand family party. I promised to stay on for a day or two, but we're busy just now and as it's the rainy season in Mallorca, I prefer to postpone a longer visit until later on. Are you going home for Christmas?'

'I don't think so. Caroline and your father both need me here. I'm going into Marlbury to do some Christmas shopping this afternoon. Only three weeks away, and I've scarcely thought about it. This coffee's good. Do you look after yourself at weekends?'

'Yes. Mrs. Lewis will always come in if I want her, but I rather like the place to myself, and if I don't feel like rustling up a meal, there's always the Woolpack Hotel.'

'Where we first met.'

'Where a dark-haired slip of a girl in a honey-coloured dress put us all under the microscope.'

'Until a dark-haired arrogant man stared her out and was like a frost in May.'

'You've never looked frosted to me.'

'Well, I don't feel frosted now,' she said, smiling at him.

'I wish I hadn't got those confounded plans to get out today. We could have had a day in the hills.'

'That would have been grand. But there will be other days.'

'Many of them, I hope,' he said, his eyes searching hers.

'And so do I. But I mustn't outstay my welcome now. Far be it from me to hold up the work of the Falkland Construction Company.'

'I can think of far more attractive things to do,' said Rolf, taking her outstretched hands and pulling her to her feet.

For a moment she stayed in his arms, and she was suddenly overwhelmed by a rush of feeling that left her trembling. She wanted to put her arms round him, to be held close. Looking up at him, she read the same message in his face, but he released her and went across to the window, where he stood with his back to her as he said, 'It's still stalemate, you know, until you make that choice.'

'I have no choice at present. Your father needs me.'

'I know. I appreciate your position. I accept that while you can help my father, your relations with Caroline must remain good and you must remain her employee. And if she suspected there was anything between us, you'd be out tomorrow. There will come a day when we're free to think only about our own lives. Then you can make your choice.'

'Is it quite impossible for you and Caroline to be friends? Or even tolerate each other?'

'The issue isn't nearly as simple as you think it is, Frankie. If I tried to explain about Caroline, it would make you angry. I know she's won your affection and trust. And as long as you're employed by her, you rightly feel that your loyalty is to her. But while your loyalty is to her, it can't be to me. If you're unable to see why, I must ask you just to accept that it is so.'

'But, Rolf, all personal relations call for some sort of compromise. Surely you could manage some sort of make-shift bridge with her.'

'You can't establish any sort of bridge, make-shift or otherwise, with a person you can't trust an inch.'

'You're too suspicious. I sometimes feel you don't altogether trust me.'

'Having a foot in two camps is a difficult feat to achieve and still retain the trust of both sides,' he said drily. 'If you can't understand my attitude to Caroline, you must accept it. After all, I have known her longer than you, and I've knocked around the world a few years longer than you have. Is it too much of a strain to accept that I might, just might, know best in this case?'

'Where people are concerned, I prefer to make my own judgment.'

He smiled, then, and said, 'Quite right, too. I like an independent mind. We'll say no more. Debate adjourned until the situation is clearer. Things are muddled now by circumstances neither of us can change at present. But the time will come. Meanwhile, we'll lock up our dreams and be severely practical. And I'll start by getting your coat.'

He held her sheepskin jacket for her, and she wondered if it was as hard for him to send her away as it was for her to go.

For the remainder of that day she was in a state of bemusement, glowing with the happiness of being truly in love for the first time in her life, shaken by the force of it, seeing a future suddenly invested with a significance and a richness that she had never dreamed of. In this mood of euphoria, there were no difficulties that could not be overcome, and that little thread of reserve which still existed in Rolf's commitment to her was so fine now that she was sure it would be swept away in the tide of their feelings for each other.

This happy state remained with her the next week, and although when she saw Caroline off on the Thursday she was aware of a sore throat and a headache which presaged another cold, nothing could dim the song in her heart.

'Hot lemon and aspirins for you,' said Caroline at the door. 'And don't go out in this shocking weather, dear.'

The rain was lashing down and a south-west gale was bending the slender conifer by the porch almost double. Jim Day-is's car had just arrived. He came into the porch carrying a large umbrella.

'Can't have you getting wet before you start, Mrs. Falkland,' he wheezed.

'How kind of you, Jim.'

'I hope you'll find your mother better, Caroline,' said Frankie.

'Thank you. Last time I was there, she did seem a lot brighter, but it's her failing sight that worries me. Until Monday, then.'

Shielded by Jim's umbrella, Caroline went out to the car, and Jim wrapped a rug solicitously round her. She leaned forward and waved as they drove off.

The gravel drive was almost awash, and a fierce gust of wind sent Frankie back into the house. But the combination of atrocious weather and sore throat weighed little against the prospect of Rolf's return that day.

It was Mrs. Filey, taking in his tea, who found Trevor Falkland slumped in his chair, and called up the stairs to Frankie.

'It's Mr. Falkland. Ring the doctor. Then come and help me.'

They got him into bed. The doctor arrived a few minutes later, his calm presence reassuring them.

'I've given him an injection. Keep him warm and quiet. I'll come again this evening. Is Mrs. Falkland here?'

'She's away for the weekend. Should we send for her?' asked Frankie.

'We'll see how he is this evening. Can't always tell. It's another slight stroke. But he pulled out of the other. I think Mrs. Falkland should be told. And his son. Rolf's away, though, isn't he?'

'He'll be back this evening.'

'Good. Don't worry. He may well pull out of this as he did the last one. You'll want some help. I'll have a word with the district nurse on my way back.'

When he had gone, Frankie said, 'I'll telephone Caroline. She should be there by now. You don't happen to know the number, Mrs. Filey?'

'No. I'll get back to the master. Poor soul! He's suffered enough.'

Frankie, unable to find the number in the notebook which was kept next to the telephone, sought Julie, who had disappeared to her room, looking scared, after the doctor had gone.

When Frankie opened the door of her room, she had it pushed back into her face by a half-dressed Julie.

'You can't come in now. What do you want?'

'Your grandmother's telephone number. I must let Caroline know what's happened.'

'Half a sec.'

She emerged a few minutes later, pulling a sweater over her head.

'I don't know the number. Why should I? I haven't spoken to my grandmother for years.'

'Well, it will be in the London directory. What's her name and address?'

'Mrs. Helston. I can't remember her address.'

'Can't remember?' asked Frankie, amazed.

'No. It's only Caro who has anything to do with her now. Grandma's only been here once, when I was a child; I used to go up with Caro to see her now and again, but I haven't been for years now, and I can't remember the address. In Clapham. A road with a church in it. That's all I can remember.'

'This is ridiculous. What about Christmas cards? Don't you send her one?'

'Caro does, from all of us, I suppose. Perhaps there's a note of the address in my father's desk. Anyway, you can get it from the London directory. She's on the phone, and the name's not all that common.'

'I'll have a look. Meanwhile, you might go and see if you can do anything for Mrs. Filey. Sit with your father for a little, perhaps.'

'It makes me ill, going in that room. Oh, this house gives me the creeps!' exclaimed Julie, shuddering. 'Anyway, I can't just now.'

She went back into her room and shut the door. Frankie, angry, searched the London telephone directory in vain, then tried telephone enquiries, but no subscriber of that name living in that area could be traced. There remained only the possibility of sending a telegram if she could find the address. Trevor Falkland had recently had out all the contents of the desk in his study and had removed a lot of papers. She had helped him re-arrange the rest. In one of the drawers was a miscellany that defied classification. Among old accounts, gardening catalogues, articles on the history of the locality, reviews of performance of the local choral society, bus and rail timetables, she remembered seeing a typed list of names and addresses which he had added to her pile of miscellaneous papers.

That might provide the answer. She tip-toed into his bedroom. He was sleeping.

'I want to go to his desk to see if I can find Mrs. Helston's address,' she whispered to Mrs. Filey, sitting by the bed.

His keys were on the chest of drawers. When she found the list, however, it related only to a record of subscribers to a church restoration fund. She went through the rest of the contents of the drawer quickly, but drew blank, except for a tattered street map of Clapham given away apparently by an estate agent of that neighbourhood. Perhaps this would jog Julie's memory. She bundled all the papers back in the drawer and returned the keys to the bedroom. The rest of the drawers contained only files relating to business matters, she knew, and were unlikely to yield the information she needed, even had she felt free to delve into Trevor Falkland's private files.

Julie's door was locked.

'I've a map here, Julie, that might help. Come and have a look.'

Julie emerged, looking annoyed.

'I've told you. I can't remember. I was only a kid when I went there.'

'She does still live in the same place, I suppose.'

'Yes. Caro and I were only recently joking about that monkey-puzzle tree.'

Frankie opened the map.

'Look, there are four churches marked here. Which one?'

'I tell you I've only a vague recollection of a church, with a field opposite. The common, I suppose. We passed the church and the house wasn't far. It had a monkey-puzzle tree in the front. But why don't you wait until Monday? Caro will be back then. Her mother's an invalid too, you know.'

'I'll see what the doctor says this evening. Rolf will be here later, and perhaps he'll have something to suggest.'

'No doubt,' said Julie, and went back into her room.

Frankie had just telephoned Rolf when the doctor arrived that evening, and he was with them within ten minutes of her call.

'When did this happen?' he asked Frankie.

'This afternoon. I telephoned just as soon as I thought you'd be back.'

'Yes. I'd just got in.'

He rested his hand on her shoulder for a moment, then went to his father's room. He soon came out again with the doctor, and they remained in the hall talking for a few minutes. When he rejoined her, he looked tired and unhappy.

'It could go either way. We can only wait and see.'

She told him about her fruitless efforts to get in touch with Caroline.

'Can you help, Rolf? Do you know the address?'

'No. Only that it's somewhere in south-west London. Do you mean to say that there's no record here? That nobody knows?'

'Only your father, I suppose.'

'He's in a near comatose condition. It can make little difference to him at the moment whether Caroline's here or not, but he may come out of it and want her. Trust Caroline to be scarce in times of trouble,' he concluded bitterly.

'She couldn't know. Unless we can think of anything better, I'll go up to London tomorrow and find her. I think I can find the house from this map and Julie's description. And perhaps it's better, anyway, for me to tell Caroline. A wire or a telephone call would be more of a shock. She can come back with me.'

'Well, it's the best idea we've hit on so far. Where's Julie? Let's see if we can pin her down more precisely.'

There was no reply to Frankie's knock on Julie's door. She looked in, and was turning away again when something odd about the room stopped her. The dressing-table looked bare. The little clock on the bedside table had gone. The wardrobe door was half open and she could see that it was empty. She went across to the chest of drawers. That was empty, too. Then she saw the note, half hidden by the dressing-table mirror.

I have gone away with Don. We are to be married tomorrow. Shall be writing to Caro about future plans.

Julie.

When Frankie returned to the sitting-room and handed Rolf the note, he looked incredulous.

'That child? I thought the affair with Birchington had gone cold. I've heard nothing of it from you for some time. Had you any idea she was still involved with him?'

'Yes. They've been secretly engaged since August.'

'And you said nothing to me about it.'

'Caroline insisted on silence, for your father's sake. She

thought it could only worry him, and Julie's eighteen. Nobody could stop her.'

'I see,' said Rolf grimly. 'And my father was to be kept in ignorance of his daughter's engagement indefinitely?'

'That was up to Caroline.'

'And between you, you denied my father any right to offer advice, to try to point out the folly of marrying a man years older than she is when she's only just out of school.'

'Caroline only did it to spare him.'

'Rubbish. She did it, as she does everything, to save herself trouble, even if Julie pays for it in the long run. I suppose she reckons that my father won't live long and need never know anything about an engagement. It will be a little harder to explain Julie's disappearance without telling him she's married, though. How is she going to fix that, do you suppose?'

'You always see the black side when it's to do with Caroline. She may have been wrong, but she was thinking of your father's health. I don't think he ought to have been worried by it, because Julie's a selfish, hard and wilful girl. At the slightest hint of trouble from her father, she would have been off with Don. She's frightened of her father. She would never face him.'

'And whose fault is that?' demanded Rolf angrily. 'She's been conditioned to it. My father's a kind man. Too kind. It's been a great disappointment to him, this barrier between him and Julie. She's his daughter. And you say he's no right to know what she's doing with her life. You connive with Caroline to relegate him to the background, a person to be humoured, deceived for his own good, treated as though he's an imbecile because he's had a stroke. It's insulting. And just to save trouble.'

'The decision was not mine.'

'You sought my advice once about Julie and Don Birchington, but kept me in ignorance when they got engaged.'

'I told you. Caroline insisted.'

'You and she certainly work well together. Anyway, it's no good tracking back now. Any idea when Julie went?'

'Between five and six, I'd say. But she must have had it planned some days ago. All her clothes have gone. She must have got them out before this. She'd enough to fill a couple of trunks.'

'We've plenty on our hands now without trying to track down Julie. Anyway, there's nothing we can do at this stage.

Another item of news for Caroline when you see her tomorrow. She probably won't be all that surprised.'

'You can't blame her for Julie's actions.'

'I blame her for not caring enough for Julie. And for heaven's sake don't tell me how kind and generous she is. She's indulged Julie, but that's not caring. It's easy. And far pleasanter to evade your responsibilities and just keep on superficial, friendly terms. A paper mother, and a paper wife,' he concluded bitterly.

Frankie was silent. She herself had felt that Caroline was altogether too casual with Julie. Charming and generous to her, but not willing to take her to London or indeed seek her companionship in spite of Julie's eagerness. For, although not a warm-hearted girl, Julie did admire her mother and have some affection for her, and Frankie had now and again sensed a hungry appeal in her manner towards her mother. But she had put it down in part, at least, to Caroline's preoccupation with her husband's health and her own ageing mother.

Rolf picked up the map again and said coldly, 'Let's keep to practical matters. You should be able to locate the house from this map, with any luck. There are only two churches facing the common. Here and here. But this one seems to stand alone, and I'd go for the other, which has a road stretching each side. The monkey-puzzle tree should be conspicuous enough, but if not, you could enquire at the houses near the church for Mrs. Helston. She's lived there for years, I believe, so should be known.'

'I'll do my best. It seems ridiculous to have no record of it, though.'

'My father would know. If he's able to talk, I'll ask him. Otherwise, we must just take a chance. I'll drive you to the station in the morning for the early train. I shall stay here for the time being. Mrs. Filey's making up the bed in the spare room for me.'

'I'm so sorry, Rolf. A wretched homecoming for you.'

'Yes. I'll go and telephone Uncle Elwyn.'

She saw little of him until the next morning, when he drove her to the station. He seemed withdrawn, and she felt unable to get near him. Her disclosures about Julie had contributed to this gulf, she feared. With her head aching and her throat no better, she did not look forward to her journey or to breaking the news to Caroline.

14
Comings and Goings

SHE found the house more easily than she expected. A few minutes' walk after passing the church brought her to a tall, Edwardian-style house, one of a row, with a monkey-puzzle tree in the garden. She snapped down her umbrella, for it was still raining, although not with the vigour of the Welsh rain she had left behind, and lifted the brass door-knocker. The door was opened by a tall, elderly woman with horn-rimmed spectacles. Frankie explained her mission, and the woman looked surprised.

'Yes, this was Mrs. Helston's house,' she said, 'but she died over two years ago. I was her housekeeper.'

'But . . . but that's impossible,' stammered Frankie. 'I was sure I'd find Mrs. Falkland, her daughter, here. I . . . I can't understand.'

'You'd better come in out of the rain.'

They were in a long narrow hall. The woman eyed her, then took her umbrella and put it in the stand, saying, 'I've just made a pot of tea. You'd best come and have a cup while we try to get things clear. You look tired. You've come up from Wales this morning, you say?'

'Yes. It's very kind of you, Mrs. . . .'

'Earnslaw. No trouble. The tea's in the pot for the drinking.'

The tea was welcome as Frankie sat in the old-fashioned kitchen, where Mrs. Earnslaw had obviously just been ironing, and listened, bewildered.

'Old Mrs. Helston's death came as a great shock. She was in quite good health, except for the arthritis that made it painful for her to get about, and she had a bit of trouble with a cataract the year before she died. Had an operation. She got over it well, though, and it was successful. It really was a shock when she went. Just died in her sleep. Kind way to go.'

'You knew her daughter?'

'Yes, she used to come here now and again. Pretty young

woman, Mrs. Falkland. Always brought lovely flowers with her, but never stayed long. We didn't see much of her. Mrs. Helston used to complain a bit, but there, young people don't have much time for the old these days, and the old lady was well looked after, though I say it myself.'

'Mrs. Falkland didn't ever stay here, then?'

'A bare hour was her stint. She stayed at a hotel in London as a rule. Brown's, I think. That was where she was the night her mother died, anyway. It was sheer luck I knew where she was that night, but the old lady had happened to mention it. Mrs. Falkland stayed on in London that week. We were the only mourners. The old lady hadn't any friends. Mind you, she had a bit of a tongue. But there, she was good to me. Left me this house so that I could let off the top floors and always have a home here and enough to live on. In fact, she left more than I expected. She was always grumbling about her investments, and spoke as though she had to be very careful, but she left her daughter quite a nice amount, as well as providing for me. Of course, she lived carefully . . .'

While Mrs. Earnslaw rambled on, Frankie tried to readjust her mind to this revelation. So it was all fiction, Caroline's visits to her mother. Just a cover to enable her to get away from Riverdale with a good excuse. She could not believe it, but there seemed no other explanation. She remembered the time she had been left to cope, with Mrs. Filey ill; the time Julie had been disappointed because her mother would be away on her eighteenth birthday; Caroline's refusals to entertain because of her commitments, which tired her so. But even then, as anger grew, she still could not quite believe it.

She drew the interview to a close as quickly as she could, for Mrs. Earnslaw was obviously curious about the circumstances which had led her astray and it was difficult to explain without embarrassment.

'I just misunderstood. Thank you so much for the tea, and your trouble. I expect I'll find Mrs. Falkland at Brown's. Silly of me.'

It sounded unconvincing to her own ears, and she escaped from Mrs. Earnslaw's curious eyes with some relief. She made for a telephone box nearby and rang the hotel, but no Mrs. Falkland was staying there. She replaced the receiver and stood staring out of the stuffy telephone box through the rain-spattered glass, conscious of feeling rather ill and very helpless. She pulled herself together, unwilling to give up her quest but wondering how she could pursue it. Then Nick's remarks about seeing Caroline go into a block of flats suddenly flashed into her mind. She tried to remember exactly where it was, but had difficulty in pin-pointing it. When she was with Nick, they were usually chattering or arguing and she left it to him to pilot the way. He knew London so well, and took short cuts which she would never have known, so that it was beyond her now to retrace in her mind that walk to the Albert Hall. She glanced at her watch. Nearly four o'clock. She would catch him at his office.

His secretary answered the telephone. No, Mr. Barbury had left at lunch-time. She understood that he was spending the weekend with friends in Hampshire. No, she didn't know the address. He would be back at the office on Monday morning. Should she get him to contact her?

'No, it doesn't matter,' said Frankie. 'I shall be back in Wales then.'

'I'll tell him you phoned,' said the polite little voice before ringing off.

Frankie emerged from the telephone box fighting the desire to give up. She would go to Kensington and try to retrace their steps. If Caroline wasn't there, she must have friends there who might know where she was. It was a forlorn chance, but she was reluctant to telephone Rolf and report failure without trying every possibility. She took the underground to South Kensington and in the dusk of that drizzly afternoon retraced their steps as best she could. In fact, on the spot, her memory proved to be better than expected, and inside twenty minutes she found herself peering through the gloom at the piece of sculpture which had caught her eye before.

There was a porter on duty at a desk in the entrance hall. A burly, cheerful man who was more than ready to talk.

'Yes, Mrs. Falkland lives here, but I'm afraid she's out today. Gone to a wedding. I'm not expecting her back until tomorrow morning.'

'I see. Has Mrs. Falkland lived here long? I was given another address,' said Frankie hastily, as he eyed her.

'Let me see, about two years, I suppose. A friend of yours, is she, or a relative?'

'I'm employed by her family, and I'm afraid I've bad news about Mr. Falkland. He's gravely ill. Could I leave a note for her?'

'Of course. I'm sorry to hear that. Her father, that would be?'

'Her husband,' said Frankie shortly.

'I say, are you sure we're talking about the same Mrs. Falkland? I thought she was a widow. My Mrs. Falkland. Perhaps you'll describe the person you have in mind,' he added, his suspicions aroused.

'Fair, very pretty, beautifully dressed and quite charming. She's forty-four, and looks years younger. Delicate build.'

'That's her, I guess. Well, it's none of my business. I know she divides her time between here and her family in Wales. I just assumed it was her parents. Separated, I suppose. She's a sweet woman. So sympathetic and kind. Some men don't know their luck.'

'You'll see that she gets this note immediately she returns, won't you? I suppose there's no chance of getting in touch with her now?'

'Afraid not. She just said she would be staying with a friend for the night. Somewhere in the Cotswolds, I believe the wedding was. A party had been arranged for this evening among a few of the wedding guests, I gathered. I'm sorry it's bad news.'

He took the note which Frankie had scribbled, and looked at her as though he blamed her for bringing bad news for his Mrs. Falkland. One more conquest of Caroline's, evidently.

Outside, it was nearly dark and home-going crowds were already queueing at bus stops. She had envisaged returning with Caroline on the train which left Paddington just after midnight. Now, as she waited to cross the road, she felt unable to face the night journey herself, and nor did she feel inclined to escort Caroline the next day. She had told her the position. Now it was up to her. With a muzzy head, legs that no longer seemed to belong to her, and a mind shocked and bewildered by the discoveries of that long, weary day, she again sought a telephone box.

Mrs. Filey replied to her first call. She told Frankie that Rolf had slipped back to the cottage to collect one or two things, and that there was no change in Mr. Falkland's condition.

'Will you tell Rolf that I wasn't able to see Mrs. Falkland, but I found her address and left a note for her which she'll get tomorrow morning. She'll probably be able to catch the afternoon train. And as I'm feeling a bit under the weather, I've decided to go home for the night and return tomorrow instead of catching the night train, but I shall come back on the earlier train in the morning.'

Mrs. Filey said that she would give Rolf the message, and

rang off before Frankie could say another word. She was probably anxious to get back to the bedside.

Frankie's mother answered her second telephone call.

'Of course, darling. Your room's always ready for you. We'll wait dinner for you.'

But by the time Frankie had got down to her parents' home in Surrey, she was in a state of near collapse and was bundled off to bed straightaway. It was a brief but fierce attack of influenza, which kept her in bed for the next two days and left her feeling weak but able to get about on the Monday. She insisted on returning to Wales on the Tuesday.

'I must. They'll need me with Mr. Falkland so ill. And I'm all right now, anyway.'

'You look washed out, dear. You need a good week's rest. When I phoned Riverdale, the housekeeper said they were coping quite well. Why not stay for a few more days?'

But Frankie returned to Wales on Tuesday morning. Jim Davis drove her from the station. She was longing to see Rolf and unburden herself to him, but she dwelt with distaste on the coming encounter with Caroline. What would Caroline say to her, and what would she say to Caroline? She had spent most of the past few days pondering on Caroline, amazed at the fantasy she had created, angry with herself for being more deceived than anybody. She had been truly fond of Caroline and anxious to relieve her of any burden.

Mrs. Filey met her in the hall and seemed glad to see her, although her dour nature precluded any enthusiastic warmth of welcome.

'I'm sorry you've had 'flu. It never rains but it pours. Today, Mrs. Falkland's in bed. Reaction from the shock of poor Mr. Falkland's condition and Julie's elopement.'

So that postponed the awkward confrontation, thought Frankie with some relief, for she was not feeling her usual robust self just then.

'And Mr. Falkland?'

'The same. Barely conscious. And with the nurse needing waiting on, too, when she's here, I've more than enough on my hands. You'll be wanting a cup of tea.'

'Don't worry, Mrs. Filey. I'll make it. Is Rolf still here?'

'Yes. He went to the office for a few hours this morning, but he's with his father now. And so is Mr. Falkland's brother, Lloyd.'

Restored by the tea, Frankie went to the study to put the street map back in the desk, anxious to see Rolf as soon as he left his father's bedside. Automatically, she began to tidy the jumbled drawer, and her task was only half done when Mrs. Filey came in with a letter in her hand.

'There was a letter for you this morning. It was waiting for you on the hall table, but Mr. Lloyd put his overcoat on top of it. I just noticed it when I hung the coat up.'

It was Nick's handwriting, and was written from his office.

Dear Frankie,

My secretary tells me you telephoned on Friday and seemed a bit thrown by not finding yours truly at his editorial desk. Sorry I missed you. Didn't know you were coming to London. I gather you're back in Wales now.

Any problems? Or has my sleuth any exciting information for me? Or were you just wanting an evening out? Whatever it was, I'm sorry that, like the cat Macavity, I wasn't there. Let me have advance notice next time.

With Christmas approaching and throwing a deadly Scrooge-like gloom over me, are you going to help me survive the ritual family gathering or will you find an excuse for staying in Wales and leave the burden to others?

At all events, keep in touch. And good hunting!

Nick.

Rolf and his uncle came out of the bedroom and she hastily folded the letter and put in the pocket of her dress as she smiled at Rolf, feeling better just for the sight of him. But his expression was arctic and her smile faded.

'So you're back,' he said. 'You can see yourself out, can't you, Uncle?'

'Yes, my boy. Poor old Trevor. A sad business,' said Lloyd, giving Frankie a wan smile and a nod as he went.

'I'm sorry I couldn't get back before, Rolf,' she began, but he cut her short.

'I want one answer from you, Frankie, and it had better be the truth, because if you lie, it can easily be disproved. Caroline told me yesterday that you were the sister of that journalist who pestered my father for an interview, and that it was he who sent you after this job. I've learned over the years not to take anything Caroline says on trust. Is it true? Just a plain yes or no.'

'Yes. It is true.'

'Well, I'll be . . .' He checked himself, then went on with a savage note in his voice which was like a knife in her heart. 'Go into the dining-room. I don't want my father disturbed.'

There, he closed the door behind them and took her by the shoulders, his eyes flashing a dangerous message. He looked capable of violence.

'You mean little cheat,' he said. 'I was right to have my suspicions that very first night. But you were clever. You persuaded me that you were on the level. Worming your way into my confidence, into my father's, so that you could drag out that old scandal and make a juicy story for a gossip column.'

'I don't know what you're talking about. I know of no scandal. Nor does my brother. He wanted to write an article about your father because he admired his work. Is that such a sin?'

'And if it was so innocent, why did you lie to me when I asked you whether you had any connection with journalism? Why did you say you came in answer to Caroline's advertisement?'

'Because Caroline insisted. She knew that your father disliked anything to do with publicity, and it seemed a harmless enough concealment since I had no ulterior motive for taking the job.'

'No? Then why lie to me?'

'I'd promised Caroline to say nothing.'

'What sort of a fool do you think I am? Your brother is a journalist who wants to make a scoop from my father's past. He sends you after this job. You lied about it because Caroline had made it clear that if my father knew of your connection, you wouldn't have stayed in this house for five minutes. I know the ways of the sensational press. They don't give up easily. Vultures, feeding off other people's misfortunes.'

'That's not true. At least, perhaps it's true of a very small section of the press, but my brother has no connection with that. He runs an art magazine.'

'Whose readers like to be titillated, no doubt. Exposing people is a popular pastime. All in the name of fearless frankness, of course. But I'm not going into that. You've lied to me and tricked me. You've tricked my father. Fortunately, I've made him take special precautions so I doubt whether you've made much progress. If you had, you'd doubtless have found some respectable reason for giving up the job before this. You're patient, I must say.'

'Rolf, you can't believe that of me. I know nothing of your father's past, except that he was a writer. I've grown so fond of him. You must know I wouldn't hurt him for the world. Or you.'

'You appeared to be starting your researches again just now. Hand over that piece of paper you pocketed in such a hurry.'

Her heart sank as she realised how Nick's letter could be misinterpreted.

'It's a private letter,' she said.

'Or something you'd come across in the desk that might offer a clue. Come on. It's open to proof. Hand it over.'

'I won't.'

He pinned her arms in a grip that hurt as he took the letter from her pocket.

'So,' he said ironically when he had read it. 'It seems rather a waste of breath trying to build up a case any longer, don't you think? Your hunting has come to an end, my girl. You're nearly as good an actress as Caroline. I'm surprised you didn't have more success on the stage. You took me in, although I did have my doubts at first. The trouble with lying, though, is that sooner or later you're found out. Tell your brother to do his own dirty work, and I'll have the pleasure of throwing him out if he's within reach. As for you, pack your bags. I'll book you a room at the Woolpack for the night, at our expense, as there's no train back tonight. I'll write out a cheque for a month's salary and let you have your insurance card. Be ready by seven-thirty. I'll drive you to the hotel. We don't want you in this house any longer.'

'Is this Caroline's decision, or yours?'

'For once, we are both in agreement.'

'Caroline has not objected before, although she knew who I was.'

'But now that my father is helpless, unable to look after his private papers or anything else, she feels a little uneasy, especially as she's noticed you going through his papers several times lately.'

'We were re-arranging the contents of the desk.'

'Quite,' he said, with the same deadly irony. 'And in any case, Caroline believes that my father won't be needing your services any more. And, being Caroline, she prefers to leave it to someone else to sack you. In this case, I am more than willing. I suppose you're surprised at your ally ditching you.'

'No, I'm not. You see, when I went to find her, I discovered that her mother had died over two years ago, and that Caroline was living in a very comfortable flat in Kensington. She had used her mother as an excuse.'

'What a house of lies this is! But I've ceased to be surprised at anything Caroline does. You chose the wrong partner. She'd have no scruples about ditching anyone who'd rumbled her. When thieves fall out . . .'

She was feeling desperately tired now, aware that she had no fight left in her. Only a hurt so deep that she had instinctively folded her arms tightly across her body as though she had to hold the pieces together. His eyes were relentless.

'Before I go,' she said quietly, 'I'd like to see your father again.'

'Spare me the hypocrisy. You were all set to cause him as much grief and worry as you could. And now you ask to see him! Haven't you any sense of shame?'

'No. Because I've done him no injury, nor intended any. And if you come with me, you can see for yourself that I don't start stealing, since you're so convinced of my criminal character,' she said with a bitter irony that matched his.

'It's a farce I don't intend to allow.'

She closed her eyes and swayed a little. Then said, with an effort, 'I realise that circumstances make some of your suspicions appear justified. But I thought that we knew each other well enough now for some trust. I thought, mistakenly, that we cared for each other. But people who care don't behave as you've done. You're hard and cruel and always think the worst of people. But your father is neither hard nor cruel, and I care for him. I won't ask any more of you but this one chance to say goodbye to him.'

'He won't know you. But you can play the game out,' he said bitterly.

She followed him into the bedroom. Trevor Falkland lay still, his face white but strangely peaceful. His head turned slightly and his eyes opened as they crossed the room. They were misty but seemed to focus on Frankie's face. She took his hand, then stooped and kissed his forehead gently. She thought she felt a faint pressure from his fingers.

Outside, she faced Rolf again.

'He won't recover?' she said.

'I doubt it.'

'I'm glad he'll never know what you think of me. He wouldn't have believed it, anyway. I'll make my own arrangements at the hotel. Don't bother.'

'As you choose. I'll have the car waiting at seven-thirty.'

She had nearly finished packing when Mrs. Filey brought her an envelope. It contained her insurance card and Rolf's cheque. The latter she tore into four pieces and put back in the envelope. She had already telephoned Jim Davis to pick her up at seven o'clock. She closed the second suitcase with some difficulty. The attack of influenza had left her as weak as a kitten, and she had to take the cases downstairs one at a time. When she looked round her room for the last time, she was in a state of numbed disbelief. It all seemed to be happening in a nightmare. Outside, a south-west gale was whipping across the garden. That ruined garden, she thought. It seemed a symbol of life at Riverdale. And the little oasis she had made in it had been a pretty futile effort.

In the hall, she left the envelope for Rolf on the table, and went to say goodbye to Mrs. Filey, who looked bewildered.

'Tell Rolf that I was able to get Jim Davis to take me to the hotel to save him the bother. And I've left an envelope on the hall table for him.'

'I'll tell him. I'm sorry you're going. So sudden.'

'Yes. But Mrs. Falkland doesn't need my services any longer,' said Frankie gently.

Mrs. Filey's lips tightened.

'She may not, but others do. No thought for anyone but herself. You look fagged out. Are you sure you're all right?'

'Perfectly, thank you. Goodbye.'

And it was the grim Mrs. Filey, who never had a soft word for anybody, who patted her shoulder and said gruffly, 'God bless you, my dear. We shall miss you.'

Jim Davis, willing and wheezy as ever, insisted on taking both cases from her, and said as he humped them out to the car, 'It's nothing but coming and going at Riverdale these days.'

The wind roared in the trees each side of them as the car moved along the twisting drive, and rain spattered against the windscreen. Out in the lane, she could see clouds racing across a pale sky, the moon appearing and then vanishing behind them again in a wild game of hide and seek. She sat there watching it in a state of numbed exhaustion.

15
Postscript

BACK at home, Frankie was forced to spend the rest of that week in bed, as her attack of influenza had returned to have a second bite at her, so that by the time she was on her feet again, Christmas was almost upon them and she deferred making any plans for the future. A curious blankness had fallen on her which made any such plans beyond her just then, and her mother insisted that she take a long holiday to build herself up.

'That wet climate and difficult job have done you no good,' she declared. 'You need a long rest. You're as thin as a rake.'

Nick was more to the point when she went to London for the day and had lunch with him. He had listened to her explanation of what had taken place with growing concern.

'And it's hit you badly. Rolf.'

'Yes. But I'm probably well out of it. A man so hard and cruel can do a lot of damage.'

'I'm very sorry, Frankie. I feel it's all my fault, sending you there in the first place. And then that silly letter. I was only joking, you know.'

'Of course I know. But coming on top of all the deception Caroline forced on me, I suppose his reaction wasn't all that unreasonable. Tolerance was never one of Rolf's virtues, anyway.'

'Wish I'd telephoned instead of writing. I nearly did, then thought that with Trevor Falkland so ill, you'd probably be tied up and nobody would want to be bothered with outside calls. If I had, I'd have found out that you were at home with 'flu instead of in Wales, as I thought.'

'Don't worry. That letter didn't really make any difference. Once I'd admitted the relationship with you, I was damned. It was all a question of intent. Nothing I could say then would have made any difference. Think no more of it. I intend to forget it as soon as I can. I'm well rid of a man who professed friendship and then believed me to be a liar and a cheat. I wouldn't plead my case now if he asked me to. Not after the way he treated me, all but throwing me out of the house.'

'Mmm.' Nick looked thoughtful as he built a little pyramid of paper-wrapped sugar cubes on the tablecloth. 'Given that there was some scandal in the past, I suppose it did look a bit fishy.'

'It seemed more like a Falkland phobia to me. What could we have done while Mr. Falkland refused to tell us anything?'

'Oh, there are ways and means of ferreting things out.'

'Does that happen, Nick? Do the press go to those lengths and hound people?'

'It has happened. Would it help if I stepped in and tried to put things in a better light?'

'No,' she said fiercely. 'He wouldn't listen. He always takes a black view of people. He'd probably throw you out.'

'Is he bigger than me?' asked Nick, grinning.

'Yes. And he's got hot Spanish blood in him. No, it's over and done with. I don't want to see him ever again. Or Caroline. I want to forget the whole set-up. Except Mr. Falkland. I was very fond of him. But there was no more I could do for him, anyway.'

'I see. Any plans?'

'Not so far. I'll think about it after Christmas. Another dead end. A new start to make. I seem to specialise in them.'

'Well, it's all experience.'

'Yes. I begin to think I've no judgment where other people are concerned, though. How could I have been so taken in by Caroline? I thought she was so good. Always thinking about her husband's peace of mind and her mother's comfort. Now I realise that she didn't care twopence for her husband, her mother, her daughter, or me. And yet she always talked as though she cared so much. I don't like being fooled.'

'There's a big difference between talk and action. You're too trusting, Frankie. You ought to keep in mind those words of Emerson:

The louder he talked of his honour, the
faster we counted the spoons.

If you could remember that, you might be spared a lot of disillusionment.'

She smiled rather wanly as she said, 'I'll remember.'

'And the worst of you idealists is that you rush from one

extreme to the other. Caroline's not a wicked character; just a shallow, self-centred one, I'd say. Out to avoid trouble for herself at all costs and to have a pleasant, superficial life. And it could be that your cruel, black-minded Rolf is in fact a man at the end of his tether. With heavy responsibilities for a father he obviously cares for and who is dying, a wily stepmother like Caroline, and a girl he feels has tricked him, I can't say I'd expect his mood to be angelic just now.'

Frankie eyed her brother's fair, handsome face with some exasperation.

'You're always so inhumanly detached, Nick.'

'I know. It's easy to be wise when you're not involved. Damaged feelings are not good counsellors. But I've always tried to point out the dangers of getting involved. You're so intense, Frankie. It's very exhausting,' he drawled, trailing his coat for her.

'And for that, you deserve everything that's coming to you this Christmas.'

'Oh lord! Don't remind me,' said Nick. 'And I'm only trying to cheer you up. That stricken-deer look in your eyes affects even my stony heart.'

At her grandmother's family Christmas party, Frankie was able to present her brother with a letter which had both saddened and comforted her.

'Read it,' she urged. 'It came yesterday, forwarded by Mr. Falkland's solicitors. He died two days after I left.'

Nick sat down behind a potted palm in the conservatory, where they had retreated from the party, and read it.

Dear Frankie,

I am arranging for this to be given to you on my death as a little thank you to a kind young woman who did so much, and so willingly, to cheer the last months of an old man's life. Our reading sessions were a delight to me, and so were the hours when you helped me to escape into the garden. You will never be a chess player, but nobody could have had a more delightful companion. Although I sometimes felt guilty that such a bright spirit should be tied to a sick old man, I knew it would not be for long. For such generosity there is no material payment, but I should like to think of you spending the enclosed on a holiday in Mallorca, which we talked about so often. Go in January or February when the almond blossom is in bloom. You may see my ghost walking in the woodland paths round the cliffs!

And if you go, Rolf's grandmother would welcome a visit. I've told her about you, and I should like you to meet her.

I hope life will be kind to you, my dear.

                    Yours affectionately,

                          Trevor Falkland.

'Wasn't that good of him?' said Frankie, her eyes shining.

'Yes. A consolation for you after the way you were dismissed.'

'And Rolf believed I could want to harm him! He enclosed a hundred pounds in ten pound notes. But that's not important. It's just knowing that the year wasn't wasted, after all. That I did achieve something.'

'Will you go? To Mallorca?'

'Yes.'

'Nice and quiet there this time of year. Do you good.'

'Mmm. I smell a nice smell here. Is it that plant or you, Nick?'

'Grandma has a nice taste in after-shave lotion. And here she comes to winkle us out. I've a ghastly suspicion that we're going to have charades.'

He stood up as his grandmother approached. Mirabel Rainwood, handsome and patrician in grey silk, studied her two grandchildren with dark blue eyes which seemed to offer a gentle rebuke.

'You're admiring my plants, I see. Have you noticed the beautiful Christmas cactus in the far corner? We're very proud of that.'

She pointed out a few more treasurers, then said, 'My family is given to hiving off in little cliques. Understandable, when I know they have items of news to exchange, but a little unmannerly. We're going to have some charades, and need your acting ability, Frankie and Nick's aura of artistry.'

'If I didn't know you better, Grandma, I'd say there was a faint suggestion of double entendre in that last phrase,' said Nick.

She smiled as she eyed his pale lavender shirt, matching flowing tie and pale grey suit.

'I admire elegance in a man, Nick. You're looking a little pale, Frankie dear. I hope you'll come along and have tea with me one afternoon next week and tell me all about your life in

Wales. Your mother tells me the job there has come to an end.'

'Yes, Grandma.'

'Were you happy there?'

'Yes. There were one or two disappointments.'

Nick's eyebrows shot up at this under-statement and he said with the lazy drawl that seemed to be more pronounced at family gatherings, 'Frankie's too trusting. She's bound to get shocks.'

'Better to be too trusting than not trusting enough, dear. I'm sorry that Jennifer and her husband couldn't be here, and that we're without Giles and Christine, too. But with Christine's boys only six months old, the journey from Northumberland would have been something of an undertaking, and Jennifer's invited them to spend Christmas at Foresters. It's nice to know that they're only a few miles from each other, and that they're all such good friends.'

'Hard to imagine our old fly-away Kit with twin boys,' said Nick, chuckling. 'They'll put salt on her tail.'

'There have never been twins in our family,' said Mirabel. 'Perhaps it's a tendency in Giles's family. I must ask him when I see him. I'm sure that with his support, Christine is coping well. But we're neglecting the party. Come along, my dears, and enjoy yourselves. Forget all the disappointments tonight, Frankie. Christmas is a time for rejoicing.'

As Nick followed his grandmother back to the noisy, crowded room, he lifted his hands in helpless supplication, and Frankie smiled. For all his mockery, she knew he was fond enough of the Rainwood tribe and had a genuine admiration for his grandmother, although he took an impish delight in trying to shock her, which wasn't as easy as one might think.

She did her best to blot out the past and enjoy herself as her grandmother had requested, but beneath all the laughter and activity, she felt hollow with unhappiness and bitterness at Rolf's treatment. She had never been in love before. It had seemed so wonderful. So invincible. Now it was like dust under Rolf's feet. She could never forgive him for that. And she could never forget.

16
For the Record

NICK was sitting in front of the fire, reading a book and making a note or two as he read, when the door bell of his flat rang twice. He frowned, not wanting to be disturbed, then went to the door. The piercing cold January wind sprang at him through the open door. A tall man stood there.

'Are you Nick Barbury?' he asked.

'Yes.'

'I'm Falkland. I had your letter. Can you spare me a few moments?'

'Come in,' said Nick with little warmth.

In the sitting-room, he eyed the newcomer critically. Frankie was right. He didn't fancy a contest with this chap. Lean, fit, and taut muscled. A good-looker too, but a bit grim.

'Are you staying long enough to use a chair?' asked Nick, waving a languid hand to the armchair opposite him.

'I don't know,' said Falkland, eyeing him sharply. 'Why did you write that letter?'

'Just to put the record straight. I don't like to have my sister falsely accused of being a cheat and a trickster.'

'Did Frankie ask you to write?'

'No. In fact, when I suggested it she indicated pretty forcibly that that was the last thing she wanted.'

'And yet you wrote.'

'I told you. I wanted to put the record straight. Whether you believe what I wrote or not is a matter of complete indifference to me,' drawled Nick, opening the onyx cigarette box by his side. 'Do you?'

'Not now, thanks. What would you have believed in my position?'

Nick considered, then said coolly, 'I can't answer that because I'm not sure what your position is. I deduce from what Frankie has told me that there's some painful episode in your father's past which has been the subject of publicity before and which you suspected might be again. I had no such knowledge when I asked for that interview with your father. I was merely interested in including him in a series of articles in my magazine called "Forgotten Authors", and wanted some biographical material from him. Perhaps if I'd suffered from the press before, and if I didn't know and didn't bother to find out the sort of journal that was asking questions now, and if I wasn't a good enough judge of character to see that Frankie, heaven help her, is as transparent as glass and would be hopeless at any devious strategy, I might have thought as you did.'

'Well, thanks for that indictment. If you'd lived with as much deviousness as I have and seen the apparently transparent and pretty face it can wear, you wouldn't pronounce so confidently.'

'Ah, Caroline.'

'You know?'

'Enough.'

'I should have looked into the class of journal you edited. I grant you that. But when I first heard of Frankie's connection with you, the time was not exactly propitious for investigations of that sort, and I had first and foremost to protect my father. It wasn't until I had your letter that I knew what magazine it was. I bought a copy. It's not a scandal sheet, I grant you, but de-bunking is very popular even with your sort of magazine, as you well know.'

'You have a case. I've said so. The point is, I had no idea there were any skeletons in the cupboard. I was, I admit, curious to know why a man with such talent as your father should have stopped writing when he was at the peak of his success. And perhaps for the record I should also add that I do book reviews for a daily. A meagre few inches a week covering three or four books. All most respectable, but I mention it because Frankie says you always take a black view and might see villainy there, too.'

Rolf eyed him thoughtfully for some moments without speaking. The summing up, thought Nick. He was annoyed at feeling less than his usual confidence vis-à-vis this man. There was grim experience etched in Falkland's face. Embattled, was the word that came to mind. Power there, too. He was older than he had expected. Early thirties, probably. He made Nick feel immature, as though, working away in his ivory tower with his books and dabbling in the arts generally, he knew nothing of the real, tough life outside. Not a comfortable companion at all, he thought, blowing a smoke ring.

'Well, I don't intend to enlighten you about any skeletons,' said Rolf at last, but Nick felt that the animosity had gone out of him, that he had satisfied himself about something. 'Is Frankie at her home?'

'No. She's abroad. Taking a well-earned holiday.'

'Where?'

'I don't know that I feel inclined to tell you. She needs that holiday. She's been clobbered enough. And she has no wish to see or hear from you ever again, according to her last statement to me on the subject.'

'I don't think Frankie needs a keeper.'

'You'd be surprised. Oh, she's got a mind of her own, and plenty of spirit. But she's such a reckless crusader, giving everybody her trust, hold out her heart on a plate to be carved up. She's still reeling from the shock of Caroline's deception. But there are small signs that she's toughening up, because your treatment seems to have got her reaching for a knife of her own.'

'I can handle that. And there will be no more clobbering. Further than that is no business of yours, you'll agree. I'd be obliged if you'd let me know where she is.'

It was Nick's turn to ponder. On balance, he was inclined to approve of this formidable character. And he was a firm believer in letting people judge for themselves. Frankie could have done a lot worse, given her disposition for being taken in. This man had no camouflage, anyway. She must know him for what he was.

'She's in Mallorca,' he said at last.

'Mallorca?' He was obviously surprised.

'Your father left her a hundred pounds and expressed a wish that she should spend it on a holiday there. You didn't know?'

'He told me he was arranging a small gift for her as a mark of his appreciation. I'm glad he did that.'

'It comforted Frankie. She was very fond of him. I had a card from her this morning.'

Nick handed him the card which was a photograph of the hotel she was staying at.

'I know it,' said Rolf. 'How long is she staying there?'

'She's been there a week. Has another two weeks to go.'

'Thank you for telling me. I won't detain you any longer. I'm sorry if I disturbed your work. I tried to ring you earlier, but was told that your phone was out of order.'

'Correct. Will you have a drink before you go?'

'No, thanks. I'm meeting some friends for dinner at eight.'

He buttoned up his overcoat, and Nick's quick eye registered the fact that Falkland might live in wild Wales, but he knew a good tailor. He passed a hand through his hair, and as he turned and the light from the lamp fell on his face, Nick noticed the drawn look about the eyes and the dark shadows underneath. He looked tired, thought Nick, dog-tired.

'Did you come up from Wales today?'

'Yes.'

'I'm very sorry about your father. I only knew him through his books, but I admired him tremendously for those. A great loss to you.'

'Yes. But a release for him.'

'I only managed to track down three of his books. There were two others to my knowledge. How many did he write in all?'

'Eight.'

'You have copies, of course.'

'Yes. They're all out of print now, and have been for years.'

'I know. I came across mine in a second-hand book shop. Couldn't understand why he'd been allowed to be forgotten.'

'It was his wish.'

As they walked to the door, Nick said, 'I don't know whether we shall be seeing each other again, but perhaps I can hope that one day you'll let me borrow the copies I haven't been able to find.'

'It's possible,' said Rolf briefly, and took his leave.

Not giving anything away, thought Nick with a wry smile as he went back to the fire. It took him some time to dismiss his visitor from his thoughts and concentrate on the book he was reviewing.

17
Mallorca

THE sandy path through the woods had been climbing for some time when it arrived at another footpath crossing it. Frankie hesitated. She was aiming to get to the wooded headland which divided the bay where she was staying from the next one along the coast. It must be the path ahead she wanted. She sauntered on.

The sun had shone every day since her arrival, and the temperature was perfect; cool enough to walk, warm enough to linger. After the cold, wet January she had left behind her, it seemed a miracle. She had spent most of her time walking along these sun-dappled, woodland paths which wound round the cliff slopes, trying to identify the pungent-smelling shrubs, letting the warmth soak into her, thinking of Trevor Falkland walking these same paths with the Mallorcan girl he had married. Some of the tiredness had washed off her during the past week, but in her heart was a core of bitter unhappiness which she tried to forget in this delightful, sun-warmed place. It would have been easier if Rolf and his father were not so bound up with Mallorca, so that she was for ever remembering what Rolf had said about the place, for ever seeing Trevor Falkland's ghost.

She pulled a flower-head from a lavender bush and rubbed its dried flowers in her fingers. There were rosemary bushes with small mauve flowers and spiny fleshy leaves, brooms, tree heathers still bearing the browned dead flowers of the previous summer. Here now, in the Mallorcan spring, the countryside looked fresh after the winter rains. In summer, she thought, it would dry up, and in these nearly deserted little bays the tourists would sun themselves in their thousands. Now, most of the hotels were closed and the hotel where she was staying had only a handful of visitors. It was infinitely peaceful along these woodland paths, the only sounds a little birdsong and the stirring of the feathery green branches of Mediterranean pines in the breeze.

The path was becoming rougher, strewn with stones and boulders, as she climbed on, until she came out to the headland and saw the blue Mediterranean far below, with a fringe of surf round the bay like a fine lace trimming. She sat down on the needle-strewn ground with her back propped against a boulder. It was so beautiful and peaceful there that the lack of peace in her heart seemed a sin.

She must put Rolf right out of her thoughts for ever. The man she had thought she loved did not exist. He had been a figment of her imagination. The reality had been a cruel man who thought the worst of everybody. It was fortunate, perhaps, that she had learned his true nature before it was too late. Such a man could bring nothing but hurt and unhappiness. She would always remember his father with kindness. The rest, she must blot out.

When she arrived back at the hotel at lunch-time, she ordered an iced orange drink and took it out on to the terrace which overlooked the sea. Sheltered here from the breeze, the sun was hot. Idly, she watched a wren flitting in and out of some agaves growing in a small bed set in the terrace. Then a shadow fell across the paving.

'Hullo.'

She jumped, spilling her drink. Rolf stood looking down at her gravely. She cloaked her amazement immediately with a stony mask, but remained speechless.

'Can I join you?'

She found her tongue.

'No,' she said decisively.

'I'm going to, for all that,' he said, drawing up a chair.

'Then you force me to go. I want nothing more to do with you. I don't know why you're here, or how you knew I was here, and I'm not interested. Just keep out of my way, please.'

'Nick told me you were here. He wrote me a letter, just to get the record straight, as he put it.'

'I'm quite sure you didn't believe it. And I wish he hadn't told you where I was. How long are you here for?'

'I haven't decided,' he said, narrowing his eyes as he looked at her.

'Are you staying with your relations?'

'No. Here.'

'Then please keep away from me. The hotel is a big one, fortunately. Otherwise, I shall leave.'

'You're not interested in talking about what happened?'

She looked at him in amazed anger.

'Have you forgotten that you threw me out of Riverdale as though I was a thief? We don't want you in this house any longer, you said.'

'Don't dramatise. Other accommodation was suggested for that night and I offered to drive you there.'

'I was, to all intents and purposes, thrown out. Nobody does that to me and gets a hearing again. I'd worked loyally for your father for a year. You and I were, I thought, good friends. And yet you treated me like that, just because you had some phobia about journalists and publicity.'

'Just because you'd lied to me,' he said calmly.

She stopped the furious words which rushed to her lips just in time. He was trying to draw her out, get her to argue. That way, he could get at her, use the power he had over her. For once, she had seen the trap Nick was always warning her about. There would be no rushing in again where this man was concerned. Her voice was cool and she managed to give him a polite little smile.

'Well, it's all academic now, isn't it? Excuse me.'

She went back into the hotel, carrying her drink.

During the next few days she became adept at avoiding him. Although the dining-room was large, the visitors occupied so few tables at one end of the room that the distance between her table and Rolf's was not as great as she would have wished, but she asked the waiter to move her chair to the other side of her table so that she had her back to him, and she took to varying the times of her meals, having an early breakfast one morning, a late breakfast the next, and since dinner was served over a period of two hours in the evening, that meal offered considerable scope for variation. She took picnic lunches instead of coming back to the hotel at midday.

On the fourth day after his arrival, he caught her up on one of the woodland paths. He must have followed her from the hotel although she had slipped out unnoticed she had thought.

'When are you going to stop this farce, Frankie?' he asked.

'No farce. Your arrogance just amazes me. Do you think I'm like a cringing dog, to come back wagging my tail after I've been kicked? I'm glad you behaved as you did. Glad I saw what you're really like. I'm through with you. I can't put it any plainer than that.'

'Nevertheless, through or not, before we close the book there are things I want to tell you.'

'Then I don't want to hear. You said everything that had to be said when you dismissed me. Just stick to that, will you, because that suits me.'

'When you stop behaving like a spitting cat, we'll have that talk. Then, and only then, you can decide and I'll accept your decision. What are you afraid of? It's a reasonable enough suggestion,' he said, putting a hand on her shoulder.

She jumped as though she had been stung and drew away quickly as she replied, 'Nothing about you is reasonable. You insult me, and call me a cheat and a liar, then expect me to behave as though nothing has happened. Reasonable? You must be crazy. And whatever I felt about you before, now I detest you.'

'You have reason, but I don't think you do,' he said quietly, taking her into his arms in spite of her struggles. She was powerless in his grasp. Lithe and agile as she was, he had a steely strength that was unassailable. She looked at him with wide, furious eyes as he tilted her chin and scrutinised her face. Then he kissed her, quite gently, running his lips from her mouth to her forehead. 'It isn't finished yet, Frankie. You must stop running away and face it. If, when I've had my say, you still want to end it, I give you my word that I'll accept your decision and you won't see me again. But I'm going to have that last word. When you're ready to listen, let me know. And let it be soon. I'm no happier than you in this situation. I'll leave you now to think about it. No good can come of any discussion while you're in this angry mood. I'm not blaming you for it. Only seeking one last chance to see if we can salvage anything from the wreckage of what meant a lot to both of us. I can't believe you won't give it to me. Think it over.'

He walked off down the path along which she had come, his dark green sweater and grey slacks merging with the dappled colours of the woodland until a sudden dip hid him completely. Frankie went on up the path, her legs shaky, her eyes blurred with tears, but determined not to give in. She had a picnic lunch and did not arrive back at the hotel until early evening after a day of fruitless heart-searching. She was simply not tough enough to take on a man like Rolf, she thought. There was no trust in him. If she smiled at a man, he would suspect the worst. If she behaved foolishly, as everybody did at times, he would show no tolerance. She would be damaged against his hardness like a puff-ball against a rock. Just now, with her confidence in her own judgment shattered by the past, she was not inclined to give anybody the benefit of the doubt.

The porter at the desk smiled at her and brought her a note. 'It came by hand this afternoon, señorita.'

She thanked him and opened it in her bedroom, unable to guess what it might be.

Dear Miss Barbury,

I have learned from my grandson that you are on holiday in Mallorca, and I should like so much to see you while you are here. Rolf's father told me about you in his letters to me, and expressed the hope that we might meet one day. It would give me great pleasure to have an opportunity to thank you personally for your great kindness to my son-in-law in the last year of his life.

May I expect you to tea tomorrow afternoon? If so, tell Rolf and he will telephone me. Please come.

Yours sincerely,

Isabella Albyon.

This put her in a quandary. She saw it as a strategic move by Rolf, but felt it would be ungracious to refuse. When Rolf came into the lounge with his coffee after dinner that night, she went to him.

'Are you responsible for this invitation from your grandmother?' she asked without preamble.

'No. I advised her not to invite you because I thought it likely that you would refuse. I didn't know she had done so.'

'Will you be there tomorrow afternoon?'

'No. I'm spending the day in the mountains with Miguel.'

'In that case, I shall accept your grandmother's invitation. Only because in the letter your father left for me he expressed the wish that I should meet her, and since I'm here through his kindness, I feel bound to respect his wishes.'

'Yes. Nick told me about the letter. I'm glad about that.'

'Your father was a very kind man. It's a pity he didn't pass that quality on to you.'

'Quite,' he said laconically. 'You were in to dinner early. Can I fetch you another coffee?'

'No, thank you. Perhaps you'll let your grandmother know.'

She left him, went downstairs to the reception hall and arranged with the porter for a taxi to take and fetch her the next afternoon. Then she went to her room. Rolf was driving her out of the public rooms. Although the lounges were large, his presence there built up a tension in her which threatened her composure, and she took to flight.

The next afternoon, the taxi took her along winding mountain roads into the centre of the island. She had not explored the country inland as yet and was surprised and charmed by its unspoilt beauty. It was like stepping back a hundred years, with the odd one-horse plough tilling the soil, the silent almond orchards, the ancient olive trees and the sheep grazing among them and bearing bells which gave a mellow ring as they moved. She remembered with a stab that Rolf had once said he would bring her to see the almond blossom. But that was part of the dream which had no reality; before she woke up to see the real Rolf. But the sight of the blossom now against the blue sky made her heart ache for the dream.

The country house which was her destination was, like all the farmhouses she had passed, built in a mellow golden stone which reminded her of Cotswold stone, but this style of architecture was Moorish not English, with small windows shuttered against the sun, and bougainvillaea tumbling over the low stone walls surrounding the courtyard in front of the house. It was set on high ground overlooking extensive almond orchards, with the mountains outlined against the sky behind.

'Until six, señorita,' said the taxi-driver with a flashing smile as he drove off.

The Spanish maid who opened the heavy door gave her a smiling greeting and led her into a cool, stone-flagged hall where a slim, white-haired woman stood smiling and holding out both hands. She spoke in a pretty voice with a near perfect English accent.

'Miss Barbury. Welcome. This is a great pleasure.'

She led Frankie through the hall and out to a small paved garden behind. Round the four sides of the garden ran a pergola covered with vines and other climbing plants which made a cool, shaded walk. In the centre, a rectangular pool shimmered and danced as a small jet of water played lazily into it. Their chairs were set in the dappled shade cast by a mimosa tree which was in full bloom and filled the garden with its fragrance. Large stone pots shaped like ginger jars were dotted about the garden, and these held geraniums in bloom, agaves, and many plants not yet blooming which she did not recognise.

This is a little paradise,' said Frankie, smiling.

The maid set out tea on the white wrought-iron table, and while Mrs. Albyon looked after her guest with the charming courtesy which Frankie had appreciated in all the Mallorcan people she had come across, she asked her about her holiday, what she had seen, where she had walked. It was not until they had finished and the maid had removed the tea things that Mrs. Albyon mentioned Trevor Falkland.

'I shall miss him. Although, since his stroke, we could keep in touch only through letters, he remained very close to me. And you did so much to brighten his last months. He wrote most kindly of you.'

'I did little enough. He seemed to me a sad man, and I often wished I could do more.'

'Yes. Life was not kind to Trevor. Sometimes it seemed that there was only one thing in his life which never failed him. His son's devotion. And even that made him feel guilty. As though he put chains on Rolf. Which, in a way, he did.'

'Yes,' said Frankie, aware of the bright, dark eyes watching her.

Mrs. Albyon's face was one which bestowed confidence, she thought. A strong face that somehow belied the fragility of the slight figure with the humped shoulders of old age. There was serenity in the face, as though she had come to terms with life, but the eyes suggested that once a more fiery spirit had inhabited the old lady.

'Prolonged self-sacrifice is not good for the character, as some might think. It has an abrasive effect. Trevor knew that because of him, Rolf had become hardened, as war hardens those who take up arms. And Rolf has been fighting a war for too many years. He started at too young an age. Trevor knew that, but could do nothing about it once his stroke brought Rolf back to his side after brief freedom.'

'You speak of a war. Against what?'

'You find Rolf difficult, perhaps?' said Mrs. Albyon, ignoring her question.

'Very.'

'The psychiatrists say that everything can be traced back to the seeds sown in childhood. There is a lot in that, although the psychiatrists see only one half of it. Man is not a helpless victim of circumstances. He has his own courage and spirit to bring to bear. But Rolf had a very unhappy childhood. There was a tragedy in his father's life which affected him when he was only eight years old. I'm not at liberty to talk of that, but there was a public scandal and schoolboys are cruel. This was when they were living in America. The unhappy affair made my daughter ill and I went to stay with her to see if I could help. Rolf used to come home from school with a black eye, bleeding knuckles, bruised face, more times than I can remember. His war started then. And eight is not a great age. He learned about cruelty then. Learned that armour was necessary. I'm not boring you?'

'On the contrary. Please go on.'

'His mother died. My dear Margarita. She was never strong, and was too gentle to cope with such trouble. Trevor decided that he must leave America for the sake of the boy, as well as for his own sake. Rolf came to me while his father returned to Wales and began to shape his life again. After he'd joined the family business and found his feet, he bought Riverdale and asked me if I would bring Rolf and look after them both while the boy was so young. Of course, I could not refuse. Rolf was as dear to me as my own children had been, and I was widowed then, and my son happily married and settled. I was at Riverdale for three years, and then Trevor married again. He was forty-two and his bride was twenty-six. A wholly unsuitable match in every way, but Trevor was trying to recapture some of the joys of his youth, I suppose. And Caroline gained a husband and a thirteen-year-old stepson. You know Caroline, of course.'

'Yes. If anybody can be said to know her,' said Frankie drily.

'A butterfly of a woman. I watched her first charm Rolf, then bewilder him, and then drive him into himself. I'll say no more. I left Riverdale as soon as Trevor married, of course. A house can only have one mistress. But I stayed on in the neighbourhood for another year until Rolf was sent to a boarding school and I felt I could do no more for him. But I knew he had another war on his hands with Caroline. She tried to divide him from his father. She never succeeded, but was able to make a good deal of trouble for him when he was young. Then, when at last Rolf was free, earning his own living in London, his father had the stroke. It was brought on, Rolf thought, by the threat of the old scandal coming to light. Anyway, Trevor asked him to come back from London, where he was working in an architect's office, and go into the family business just temporarily, so that he could be at hand for what Trevor firmly believed were the last months of his life. If he had known he would live for another five years, I don't think he would have asked it of Rolf, because he knew how things were between him and Caroline. Rolf refused to live at Riverdale ever again, but he went back to Wales and kept a close watch over his father. The price in frustration has been high, I think.'

'Yes. There were so many undercurrents at Riverdale to contend with, too. I didn't realise that fully until quite recently.'

'A house of lies, Rolf has called it. And he's lived with it on and off for the best part of eighteen years.'

'And it's destroyed his trust in people. Made him hard.'

'Made him wary, shall we say? Although he may appear hard, he's really a man of deep feeling. Otherwise, would he have devoted himself to his father as he did? And to me he has given love, too. But I agree that it has made him a hard man to know. He's learned to conceal his heart. Trevor's dearest wish was that Rolf should marry a woman who would give him all the warmth he had missed in his life. Trevor experienced that kind of happiness with my daughter. He hoped that Rolf would experience it, too, one day. He has much to give, to the right woman. But he is no angel, of course. A lot of pride, a dominating streak. Not a reed to be bent to any woman's will. Trevor thought that you might, perhaps, be that woman. You had depth enough, and warmth enough, and character enough, he said, to take on his formidable son. And he thought that there was some bond between you, although neither of you made it known to him. He just sensed it.'

'And he asked you to tell me about Rolf's life?'

'If I thought fit when the opportunity arose. He felt it would help you to understand things in Rolf which could be a stumbling block between you. But Rolf seemed averse to my inviting you and his expression forbade me to probe. I could see things were not smooth. But I took a chance. Now, it is none of my business any longer. I have done as Trevor wished. You must forgive me if I've assumed too much, talked too much about someone who is perhaps no more than an acquaintance to you. Trevor was always inclined to be a little romantic.'

'I'm grateful to you, Mrs. Albyon. It has explained quite a lot to me. But things are, as you say, not smooth, and I can't be more explicit. I just . . . don't know. I need to think.'

'That is well. Marriage is a serious undertaking. Whatever you decide, Frankie, it has been a pleasure to meet you, and to be able to thank you for all you did for Trevor. I hope, if you are in Mallorca again, you will not fail to come and see me, and we can talk about less complex matters than the Falkland character. And do not worry, my dear. Your heart will tell you, in the end, what it is right to do.'

Frankie was hardly aware of the taxi ride back, or of bathing and dressing for dinner. Round and round in her mind went the arguments. And in spite of the better understanding of Rolf which his grandmother had given her, she still could not forget his contemptuous voice and his insulting words. 'As for you, pack your bags . . . We don't want you in this house any longer . . . You mean little cheat.' She could never forget them.

He came in late to dinner that night and she was leaving the dining-room as he came in. He held the door open for her politely. She waited for him in the lounge. There was dancing there that night and he took his coffee to the corner furthest from the three-man band. He had changed his tactics and was leaving it all to her. She went across to him and said briefly, 'We'll have that final talk tomorrow morning, Rolf.'

'Certainly. I've hired a car for the week and thought of driving into the mountains tomorrow and then walking. As good an opportunity to talk as any.'

'I wasn't aiming to make it an excursion.'

'I'll put down at any point you choose when we've finished,' he said ironically. 'At nine-thirty?'

'Very well.'

'Aren't you going to stay for the dancing?' he asked, as she turned away.

'No. I don't feel in a dancing mood. Goodnight.'

Dancing indeed, she thought, as she walked upstairs to her room. Once let him get his arms round her, and she was lost, as he very well knew. And she had no intention of being lost. But he was effectively spoiling her holiday. Something must be settled one way or another tomorrow.

18
The Last Crusade

SHE slept very little that night, but fell into an uneasy doze as daylight was breaking, so that she was late for breakfast and missed Rolf in the dining-room. When she emerged from the hotel five minutes late for their rendezvous, he was waiting by the car.

'I've decided to spend the day at Puerto da Andraitx, Rolf. If you'll drop me there, that will give you time to say what you wish to say. It won't make any difference, though. My mind is made up.'

But instead of keeping parallel with the coast, he drove inland.

'This isn't the way to Puerto da Andraitx, is it?'

'It's one way. I thought we'd leave the car at a little village about three miles inland and walk down to the coast from there. I don't like talking while I'm driving, particularly with a hired car I'm not familiar with.'

'I don't want a three-mile walk. You can't have all that to say.'

'I'll leave you to finish the walk on your own if that's your wish after I've said what I have to say. It's a lovely walk. No hardship.'

Silence lay between them while he drove along the twisting mountain road and finally drew up at the end of a small village street.

'We go down that lane on the left. I can leave the car here.'

The narrow lane wound along between almond orchards. The sun was shining and the birdsong reminded her of an English spring.

'First, Frankie, why is your mind made up against me to the extent that you're not willing to listen to anything I have to say?'

'Because I know that we can only make each other unhappy.'

'You didn't think that before. On Cader.'

'I didn't know you then. Don't think I'm just flouncing off in a rage. I've thought about it deeply during the past days. But you treated me so cruelly for what was really not a major crime, even if I had ever had in mind trying to break through your father's objection to publicity. You see, I'm not good at coping with cruelty. And if you could be like that over something that wasn't all that bad, what would you be like if anything serious ever cropped up? No tolerance, no understanding, no trust. If I were tough and could shout back and fight you with your own weapons, and get it out of my system, it would be better. But I can't. Cruel words keep on twisting inside me like a dagger, and the wound gets worse, not better. I'm not boasting of it. It's just that I know my weakness. People can flay me with a cruel tongue. It finished my acting career. It could finish me in other ways, too.'

Her voice shook and she was very near to breaking down then. His quiet voice steadied her.

'I understand. I wish you'd said that before, instead of just spitting and running away. But that was all part of your fear that I'd override you, I suppose. That I'd make love to you, and your mind would lose the battle.'

'Yes. My emotions too easily rule my mind. Nick's always trying to cure me of it. But it could be disastrous for both of us in the long run, if that happened. I've come to the conclusion that you and I are just not right for each other.'

'I love you, Frankie. I was mistaken, perhaps, in thinking you cared for me.'

'Love me! How can you say that after the way you treated me?'

'Would I have been so savage if I hadn't cared? But let's not get into an argument. I want to tell you why it didn't seem a trivial deception to me. I couldn't tell you before, but it can't hurt my father now. All the same, I'd rather it went no further. His name means something to his family. Did my grandmother say anything of the past?'

'Only that there had been a tragedy in your father's life.'

'In his thirties, he was a well-known writer in America. He was an idealist, you know. And, like you, sensitive. He had a keen sense of justice and could be fierce in its cause, though, and when an influential critic carved up a writer and a friend whose work my father admired, he took up his pen and wrote a scathing indictment of that critic. And he could be acid with his pen. That critic never forgave him. And his turn came. I was only a kid at the time, and never knew the whole truth until I was twenty and my father told me all about it and showed me the documents in the case, which he'd kept all those years. With a kind of bitter masochism, he used to get them out and go over them again. It was those papers I thought your brother was after.'

He stopped to draw her into the side of the lane to allow a donkey-cart to pass. It was piled high with green branches, fodder of some kind, she thought. Rolf exchanged a Spanish greeting with the dark-skinned old man, who jogged on past them at a leisurely pace.

'My father was a hopeless businessman,' he went on. 'He put up some money for a friend of his to form a company and became a sort of honorary director. He knew next to nothing about the business and wasn't interested. He lived for his writing. But the man was an old friend who'd done him a good turn once. The company got into difficulties, and tried to buy their way out with a false prospectus which caught quite a few investors. No need to go into the details, but my father's friend, two other directors and my father were all indicted for fraud, and stood trial. It became apparent from the evidence that my father had merely been an ignorant bystander. But he had been guilty of criminal negligence, the judge said, which had contributed to the defrauding of a good many people. It was true, I suppose. My father took no part in the company's affairs, but he had helped to finance it and his name appeared on the notepaper as a director. That was the extent of his participation. He got off with a hefty fine. The others went to gaol. It was not exactly a happy time for any of us, and it helped to kill my mother.'

Frankie remembered the black eyes and the bruises, and could imagine the life he had led at school.

'But as if my father had not paid enough, the critic had his revenge and went to town on the publicity. My father's books were sensitive, idealistic, with a mystic flavour. Hypocrite was the most polite term the said critic had for him. Trevor Falkland was lampooned mercilessly. And he also reaped a nice harvest of vicious anonymous letters.'

'How can people be so cruel!' said Frankie.

'Nobody likes losing money,' said Rolf cryptically. 'And revenge is sweet. My mother died after a short illness. Officially, of pleurisy. I came here to live with my grandmother for a year while my father gave up his career as a writer, returned to Wales and joined the Falkland Construction Company. He never wrote another book. He was completely shattered by all that had happened, and he never forgave himself. Ignorance was no excuse, he said. And he'd brought misery on all of us. I could never get him to put it behind him. I begged him to let me burn those damned papers, but he never would.'

'Did his family in Wales know about it? Caroline never gave any hint.'

'Nobody knew there. His books never had much success in the U.K. His work was relatively unknown in Wales. All the family knew was that he'd given up writing as a bad job and had come home. There hadn't been much contact between them. He'd left Wales when he was twenty, lived in America, had married a Mallorcan girl. To them, he was a foreigner who had seen the light and returned to his proper home in the end. I was determined at all costs that the old scandal should never be known here. He'd paid enough. That was the reason for my phobia, Frankie.'

'Yes. I can see. And you thought that Nick . . .'

'What else could I think? My father as a writer had ceased to exist. His books were all out of print, and he'd never been known here, anyway. Why else should a journalist want to interview him, find out about him, if he hadn't got wind of that old story?'

'And Nick convinced you otherwise?'

'Yes. I got hold of a copy of his magazine. It seemed a decent sort of publication. From the meeting I had with him, I concluded it was only my father's books he'd been interested in. I thought he was honest.'

'But not me?'

'My dear, aren't you letting your pride have a bit too much rein? Twice you lied to me about what brought you to Riverdale?'

'Not directly. I let you draw the wrong conclusions, I agree.'

'Isn't that the same thing?'

'Yes, I suppose so.'

'And you hid Julie's engagement from me. Don't you see, Frankie? All my life I've lived with deception from Caroline. Small deceptions, large deceptions. Like a web. When I thought I'd fallen in love with a girl of Caroline's sort, and that she'd come to Riverdale under false pretences to help her brother achieve a journalist's scoop from my father's past, I just saw red. There had already been an attempt to blackmail him five years ago. Just before his stroke. Fortunately the police were on the tail of this particular character and nabbed him for other attempts at blackmail before he could talk. But do you wonder that I was suspicious? I couldn't afford to take chances. And that it should be *you!* Well, I just let it rip. I'd like to say that if I hadn't been short of sleep and full of bitterness for the wretched life my father was just giving up, I'd have been less cruel. But I can't be sure that it would be true. I was cruel to you because it was such a cruel blow to me. For that, I can only ask your forgiveness.'

She stumbled over a small piece of rock on the grass verge and he caught her.

'You're not looking where you're going,' he said gently, and she was crying in his arms.

He said nothing, just held her, until the storm of sobbing subsided. It was the culmination of weeks of tension and unhappiness, when she had shed no tears but had been racked with grief. Now it all had to come out. He handed her a handkerchief when at last she lifted her face from his shoulder.

'Mop up. You're shaken to bits. Come and sit on the wall and get your breath.'

They sat on a low stone wall that bounded an orchard of olive trees. He kept quiet while she collected herself. The bells of some sheep grazing in the orchard were the only sounds to break the silence.

'I'm sorry about that,' she gasped. 'Something gave. How could we damage each other like this?'

'Nothing but unhappiness ever came from Riverdale. I've got a superstition about the place. Its ruined garden was a fitting comment. A place of decay and corruption. And that old disaster lived on. It seemed as though we'd never stop paying for it. And I was afraid that in the end it had lost me the best thing that had ever come into my life. Has it, Frankie?'

'No. If I'm the best thing. I don't feel much of a blessing just now. If I'd known it all, I'd have understood better.'

'Well, we know it all now. Shall we put it behind us and make a new start?'

'Yes, Rolf.'

'And be married very soon?'

'Yes. Just hold me and let it sink in. I'm going to be wonderfully happy soon, but just now, I'm too near the crack-up,' she said, her voice still quivering a little.

She leaned her head against his shoulder and watched the sheep under the ancient olive trees. A shepherd was sitting on the wall at the far end of the orchard, a sheep-dog at his feet. It was like a biblical scene, she thought. If she had not been so concerned with her own wounds, she might have thought more of his. And when she remembered the life he had led since he was a child, she ached now to bring some warmth and trust and happiness into his life. To that end, she would give everything she had it in her to give. Another crusade, Frankie? She could hear Nick's voice. But this would be the most worthwhile crusade of her life.

Rolf's hand moved gently in her hair, and she was glad of his quiet kindness. Looking up at him, she realised that they were both exhausted by the strain of the previous weeks. They needed a little time to realise that it was over.

'We shall be happy, Rolf,' she said simply.

They both lost all sense of time as they sat there, saying little, in a rapt mood of peace after storm. It was Frankie who came down to earth first.

'I'm hungry,' she announced.

'Reassuring, if prosaic. As a matter of fact, I feel a bit hollow myself. I know a good restaurant in Puerto da Andraitx. We'll celebrate.'

And they did. And afterwards, they climbed a wooded slope above the little fishing port and were lost to the world for some hours. Walking back to the car as the sun began to dip, Rolf became practical.

'Would earlyish in March suit you for our wedding?' he asked, removing some pine needles from her hair.

'A month's time. Why linger, though? I only want a quiet wedding, don't you?'

'Yes. I'm starting in partnership with Martin Teviot at the beginning of April. I felt I wanted two months' break to sort myself out. I've put my cottage up for sale.'

'Where are you living now, then?'

'In a hotel at Richmond. Quite comfortable. We could both live there while we look for a house. Where do you fancy? London or green belt? It will have to be within reasonable reach of London. Otherwise, the choice is yours.'

'I was born in the Surrey hills, and although I don't want to be too much in the lap of my family, I would prefer the country in Surrey or Sussex for our home.'

'Suits me. I wondered whether you thought of returning to acting.'

'No. I've a job more suited to me in prospect, and I intend to give it all my modest talents so that it will be my best achievement yet.'

'Would you be referring to our marriage?'

'What else? Our home will bear no resemblance to Riverdale, I promise you.'

'I should think not. I'll do my best, too, Frankie. I've never thought marriage was a soft option. But it will be good to put roots down together and build a worthwhile life. And if we have children, give them a decent, happy home.'

'And never be lonely again. You'll be doing the work you want to do, and whatever difficulties we come up against, they'll be shared. What's happened to Riverdale, by the way?'

'Caroline put it up for sale the day after the funeral. She went to London.'

'Was she as delicate as she made out, and looked?'

'I've only ever known Caroline ill at strategic moments,' said Rolf drily. 'But I refuse to look back. Do you know where I want to take you for our honeymoon?'

'Andalusia, at a guess.'

'Yes. Granada, to be more specific. The most romantic city in the world. In March it will be at its loveliest, to my way of thinking. And we can explore the wilder mountainous regions from there, if you're not tired out by other activities,' he said, his lips twitching.

'I'm not easily tired,' she said, her eyes dancing.

'So I've noticed.'

When they arrived back at the hotel, a letter was waiting for her. She showed it to Rolf at dinner that night, when they shared a table, and watched his face in a state of hopeless infatuation as he read it. She had never seen him happy before, as he had been that afternoon. Blazingly happy, with a vital spark in him which lifted her spirits to an intoxicating state and landed her in thrall to him as never before. She saw his lips twitch as he turned over the page. Nick had written:

Dear Frankie,

I was glad to have your card. I trust I am not in the doghouse now for putting one, Rolf Falkland, on your trail. I think he means business. If you should be foolish enough ever to contemplate marriage, you could do worse. I've always thought you needed a strong arm behind you. With your propensity for being taken in, I've feared that you might make a disastrous choice. R.F., though a somewhat formidable character, reassured me a little about your judgment. But far be it from me to encourage thoughts of matrimony. A terrible trap. The thing is, are you strong enough to resist the bait? I fear not, in which case R.F. has my approval. In any case, I don't think you stand an earthly.

You may be interested to hear that I spent a most enjoyable half hour yesterday having tea with Caroline. Bumped into her outside her flat, and she invited me in. A delightful flat, bursting with spring flowers. She spoke very kindly of you. Was sorry she was ill when you left. Asked me to convey her kind regards! She has a friend who runs a little dress shop in Kensington, and C. takes an interest in it. No hard work, you realise. Just an interest. She needs it to get over the loss of her husband and Julie. But she had seen Julie and her husband, and her dear children were so happy (!) that she couldn't feel cross with them. Etc., etc. I must say I found it all most amusing in view of what I knew. Pure fantasy. It's really quite an achievement to create a fantasy world exactly to suit your comfort and tastes and keep the real world at bay. Things are what Caroline wants them to be. You've got to hand it to her.

By the way, a kind publisher has actually accepted my book for publication.

Yours aye,
Nick.

Rolf smiled wryly as he handed the letter back to her.

'I rather take to Nick. He's spot on about Caroline. Easy to be amusing about it, of course, if you're just a spectator.'

' "The dear children". Have you ever known anybody less like a dear child than old wolf, Don Birchington?' demanded Frankie.

'Hardly. But he relieved Caroline of the responsibility of a daughter. She hated responsibility. Dodged it all her life.'

'You don't think there was any man behind her move to that flat?'

'No. She's a woman incapable of loving anybody but herself. She wouldn't object to a few elderly admirers perambulating around, but nothing more, I'm sure. A nice, easy, superficial life of shops, theatres, parties, snuggling like a kitten into the cushions of her cosy flat. I couldn't stand her because she was phoney. I don't know at what stage my father saw through her act, but he had to accept it, as he'd accepted so much. After all, she was a decorative piece, and once you rumbled her, you robbed her of any power to damage you. We never discussed her. But let's forget Caroline. We don't have to worry now. She can play-act for others. We're free. I'm free. And more than a little drunk at the prospect.'

'Me, too. And after all, if it hadn't been for Caroline, we should never have met.'

'Then in that case, I'm even willing to drink a toast to her,' said Rolf, lifting his glass of champagne.

'Coupled with success to Nick's book. I'm so glad he's made it at last.'

They danced that evening, the state of intoxication still with them. Afterwards, Frankie fetched her coat and they walked along a narrow twisting road to the next small, wooded bay. At nights, as soon as the sun set, the temperature plunged, and it was a cool, crisp air which met them. It was a calm night, with the moon sending a glittering path over the sea and making a white stone house on the cliff edge stand out like everybody's dream of a fairy castle in Spain. They stopped to admire the black wrought-iron gates, the curved arches, the Bougainvillaea falling over the low white wall.

Down in the little bay where the waves broke softly, Rolf took her in his arms.

'Moonlight, the Mediterranean, the girl you love. It's odd how all those things that sound so corny are so wonderful when you actually have the luck to experience them. This coast will be overrun with candy-floss tourism in the summer, but just now, at this moment of time, there's magic here.'

'I love your island, Rolf. We must come back, often. Your father loved it, too. He found magic here with the girl he loved. He would be happy about us. You knew he wanted it?'

'From a few subtle remarks, yes.'

'I wish he knew.'

'My grandmother, a woman of simple faith, would say he does.'

'Well, this island will always be to me the place where he found his love, and I found mine. It will always be dear to me.'

'History repeating itself. My father and mother. And us.'

But their sequel would be happier, thought Frankie. It was a vow that she had made to herself. Not only because of her deep love for Rolf and the desire to make up for the past, but because, too, it would seem like a compensation to Trevor Falkland for his ruined life. If his ghost walked these wooded slopes now, he would be happy for them.

Romance in the tradition of Lucy Walker

IRIS BROMIGE

AN APRIL GIRL. Philippa and Rupert's love was a fragile thing, needing encouragement to grow. But something in Philippa's past held her back—and Lucille Pallys was quick to take advantage of it.

THE MASTER OF HERONSBRIDGE. Hoping to prove her independence, Charlotte left her wealthy parents to work for the Staverton family. But soon she was intimately involved in their traditions, their rivalries—and their romances.

ONLY OUR LOVE. Linda was sure her hated relatives were deliberately disgracing her, but she wasn't sure if her beloved Angus would see it that way.

THE TANGLED WOOD. Alison thought she had a chance for a new life—but an inherited feud with her nearest neighbors threatened her newly found confidence and her hopes for love.

THE STEPDAUGHTER. Bridget was no kin to the wealthy and tightly knit Rainwood family, and so she never felt completely accepted—especially when they began to spread rumors about the man she loved—the man who'd married her cousin.

THE YOUNG ROMANTIC. It seemed as though Robin knew all about what she did before she even had time to tell him herself. Something—or someone—was undermining their engagement—and she was totally helpless.

THE ENCHANTED GARDEN. Julian's garden had always been Fiona's refuge when her world became too harsh. She loved him dearly, but to him she was just a child—and Fiona thought the only way to bring him to his senses was to leave him.

THE CHALLENGE OF SPRING. When Tony died, Delia took refuge in her grandparent's peaceful country home, hoping to fill the void. But soon she realized she was in love with their neighbor, Gavin Dilney—a love whose destiny hinged on someone else's despair.

ALEX AND THE RAYNHAMS. Alex was dazzled by the gay, carefree life of the wealthy Raynham family—and especially handsome Bruce. But Nigel, the family outcast, constantly warned her away. Was there more to the Raynhams than met the eye?

THE FAMILY WEB. Dinah's grandfather is used to wealth and power—and he is spinning a web around her—slowly maneuvering her into hating the one man she can trust—and marrying the man she hates most. . . .

To order by mail, send 80¢ for each book (covers postage and handling) to Beagle Books, Dept. CS, 36 West 20th Street, New York, NY 10011.

"Rarely has a writer of our times delved so deeply into the secret places of a woman's heart."—*Taylor Caldwell*

DENISE ROBINS

THE UNTRODDEN SNOW. A young girl's discovery that she was adopted sends her on a flight to Switzerland, where she finds love—and the mother who abandoned her!

LOVE AND DESIRE AND HATE. Fran suspected she was losing the man she loved to another woman—but if she fought back, she might destroy them all. . . .

YOU HAVE CHOSEN. When Toni came into a small inheritance, her roommate Helena offered to strike a bargain: for half the money, Helena would sell Toni her fiancé!

THOSE WHO LOVE. Convinced that he was a dying man, Noel persuaded Peta to marry him, hoping to repay her kindness with the money he would leave her after his death. But then Noel recovered. . . .

BRIEF ECSTASY. Hidden beneath a heavy wedding veil, Rosemary took Mercedes' place and married Pablo in her stead. It was to save Mercedes from a forced marriage, But Rosemary was now in the same predicament —Pablo refused to let her go. . . .

INFATUATION. He was handsome, dashing, and an actor—the heart throb of every girl in the neighborhood. Who could blame her for marrying such an attractive stranger . . . ?

THE UNLIT FIRE. Andra had sworn to marry Trevor— a promise she could not break—even though she would be his wife in name only. . . .

SHATTER THE SKY. She had married him out of desperation and despair—although she loved another man— a dead man. Now on her honeymoon she was falling in love with the dead man's cousin. . . .

CLIMB TO THE STARS. Jane's beautiful cousin Sonia wound the man Jane loved around her little finger—and Jane could only stand by and watch. She had sworn never to reveal Sonia's secret—a secret that would bring him back to her!

To order by mail, send 80¢ for each book (includes handling and postage) to Beagle Books, Dept. CS, 36 West 20 Street, New York, NY 10011.

Beagle Gothics

Novels of romantic suspense . . . of damsels in dire danger . . . each with an eerie twist and a dark hint of the supernatural

EVELYN BOND

THE GIRL FROM NOWHERE. She spoke a prehistoric language while in a trance, and her strange ability threatened to destroy them all!

THE DEVIL'S FOOTPRINTS. A sinister medium singled her out for a dire prophecy of doom, warning her to leave the ship or she would face death . . .

DARK SONATA. Was Sekhar a charlatan or the possessor of supernatural powers? Either way, she was still the target of his revenge . . .

EDWINA NOONE

The Craghold Chronicles . . . stories set in the unique setting of Craghold—the unforgettable old house of many secrets . . .

THE CRAGHOLD LEGACY #1. Anne came to Craghold for a rest, but she was constantly upset by the suave manager who shunned the sunlight and the porter not everyone saw . . .

THE CRAGHOLD CURSE #2. Theresa's father dragged her out of their home in the middle of the night —to Craghold. But before she could discover his secret reason she was carried into terror . . .

THE CRAGHOLD CREATURES #3. To Cornelia, it was the perfect setting for her company's next chiller movie. To the things that inhabited the house, it was the perfect setting for the nights of horror to come . . .

To order by mail, send 80¢ for each book (includes handling and postage) to Beagle Books, Dept. CS, 36 West 20 Street, New York, NY 10011.

Elizabeth Seifert

has written 64 novels of men and women of modern medicine, each one with her unique combination of emotional understanding and medical knowledge.

THE BRIGHT COIN. As soon as she had broken her engagement with Dr. Joel Roberts, Rainy regretted it. But before the quarrel could be patched up, Donna came to work for Joel—and the predatory city girl knew in a second that a lonely, rich, young country doctor was no match for her wiles!

THE DOCTOR'S SECOND LOVE. As soon as Dr. Tom Kelsey joined the giant hospital as head of a controversial department, a mysterious persecution began. Did it have anything to do with the growing attraction he felt for a lovely colleague—a love hampered by a barrier of memories . . . ?

THE DOCTOR TAKES A WIFE. Dr. Phil Scoles emerged from a terrible crisis with a "second chance" to follow his dream of research. But the research center held another dream—the lovely and troubled Page Arning. In loving her, he faced the greatest challenge of his emotional life—and his career.

DOCTOR IN JUDGMENT. Not yet ready to marry her childhood sweetheart James, Mary Ruble became involved with a sophisticated crowd whose scandalous antics rocked the town. Dr. Ruble, Mary's beloved father, reacted with anger and mistrust—accusing his daughter of a terrible transgression. . . .

SUBSTITUTE DOCTOR. It seemed that Dr. Garde Shelton followed too closely in Dr. Kurt Lillard's footsteps after Kurt was sent to prison on a murder charge. First Garde took over his position at the hospital—now he was taking over Kurt's relationship with the lovely Stanfield sisters. . . .

To order by mail, send $1.00 for each book (includes postage and handling) to Dept. CS, Beagle Books, 36 West 20 Street, New York, NY 10011.

KILDARE AND GILLESPIE

The most famous medical team in fiction—known world-wide from books, movies, and television—brought to life by the incomparable

Max Brand

YOUNG DR. KILDARE. One living . . . one dead—that was Jimmy Kildare's score his first night on ambulance service. And both threatened to stop his medical career before it had started!

DR. KILDARE'S TRIAL. With death seconds away, Kildare had to decide on the right treatment to save the girl's life. He made his choice—and she lived. But she was crippled, and blamed it on Kildare. . . .

DR. KILDARE TAKES CHARGE. Medwick was a town without doctors. Kildare knew six young doctors who needed a start—and like a whirlwind he bullied, stole and blarneyed until he had the supplies needed and the grudging consent of the town—but then the plan went sour. . . .

CALLING DR. KILDARE. "It's jail for a doctor who works outside the law," Kildare told the stunning redheaded girl. But he knew that once the police had her brother, he was headed for the electric chair. Kildare knew what he had to do. . . .

THE SECRET OF DR. KILDARE. Kildare was the only hope to save Nancy Messenger's life and sanity—and the case was a passport to a life of riches and ease. But Dr. Gillespie needed him too—to carry on the work after he was gone. Kildare chose to abandon Gillespie . . . or seemed to.

DR. KILDARE'S CRISIS. Nurse Mary Lamont sought Kildare's help in getting her brother's ideas a hearing before the powerful financier who owed Kildare a favor. But Kildare's first look at Douglas told him something was dreadfully and strangely wrong. . . .

DR. KILDARE'S SEARCH. An accident victim *had* to meet a deadline—but where and with whom he couldn't reveal. Kildare had stuck his neck out once before—now he had to stake his career on a wild-goose chase that just might save a man's life. . . .

To order by mail, send $1.00 for each book (includes postage and handling) to Dept. CS, Beagle Books, 36 West 20 Street, New York, NY 10011.